MASQUERADED

Act One

by

ALEXIS DEES

Cover design by Romi Lindenberg / RomiLindernberg.com
Book design by Alexis Dees

This book is a work of fiction. Names, characters, places, and incidents either are products of the author's imagination or are used fictitiously. Any resemblance to actual persons, living or dead, events, or locales is entirely coincidental.

Alexis Dees
Visit my website at www.CarouselOfChaos.com
Printed in the United States of America

First Printing: September 2020
Carousel of Chaos

ISBN- 978-0-578-72099-9

"I feel for a society that no longer embraces wonder."

— Johnathan Lee Iverson

CONTENTS

SCENE ONE

The unfathomable transpires before your very eyes, feeding your deprived imagination a little taste of awe and wonder. Taunting and laughing in the face of the Enlightenment thinkers and blowing to pieces the findings of precious scientific research. One law the human mind is succumbed to instinctively, is curiosity; the simple need to discover. The need to explain. The need to have logical justification as to what occurs on these grounds. But there is no logical justification! There is no sensible explanation! This is how the world works around us. Gloating at our ignorance and lack of understanding. But if you believe you can, and you're willing for a challenge then step right up to this gate and know that you cannot back down. Your exit is your knowledge, and the mundane is now left behind."

Maniacal laughter complimented the all too familiar tenor voice laced with humor. This was all, clearly, hilarious to him. There was a touch of arrogance in his speech, exposing how he saw people in regular society. *Lesser than.* Nevertheless, the taunting still lured all who listened. This only stroked his ego even further.

As familiar as we were to each other, he had no name that I knew of. This was another part of his game in *my* dream. My mind had likely gone askew. But nonetheless, I called him the Ringmaster. That's what he appeared to be.

He knew quite well, however, who I was. This being to my disdain. The Ringmaster was fond of humoring himself at my expense.

The introductory monologue he did was always accompanied by a grand, albeit unsettling montage sort of preview to the circus. A series of disorienting strobe lights segued from one creepy scene to the next. A few to mention were of antique dolls with their porcelain skin cracked and dresses slightly torn, clowns whose lips were colored with blood rather than paint, and those of magicians performing gruesome tricks that turned out to be all too real.

It was a lovely little preshow to the even more horrid main show. Perfectly topped off with the sound of a haunting calliope playing slowly in the distance. I always found its sound to be annoying despite my love for less morbid circuses. It sounded as if it needed to be put out of its misery.

After the opening concluded, the Ringmaster would then appear, leading the way into an old, abandoned circus. On the subject of things that need to be put out of their misery, the poor place looked like in its day sixty or seventy years ago, it would have been a sight to behold. Now? Its once vibrant colors and wonderous atmosphere changed to the perfect set for a horror movie.

The Ringmaster would saunter into the forming fog, knowing that I would follow. He would then look over his shoulder with a grin on his face as if he were making sure I was right behind, despite knowing fully well that I'd follow. That would be the point I'd take my first step. Entering the circus and knowing the entry gates behind me would fade away.

His resounding chuckle echoed through the fog, in part acknowledging my presence and to cue that the dream was not "scripted" from this point on. The aforementioned scenario that played out was always the same. It was after his acknowledgement that the dream would then vary. It never panned out the same way twice from this point on.

His back was facing me as he rounded a tent and disappeared into the midway. I stared at the crimson red fabric of his topcoat. My being only five-six in comparison to his six-two or so, I could only stare squarely at his back. Without a doubt he could sense my glare as I debated what I wanted to say, but it didn't matter to him—just whatever he wanted to show me.

On our way down the midway, we crushed underfoot littered popcorn and stuffing that floated in the wind from mutilated stuffed animals. The wooden frames of the games and concession stands were rotting in addition to the paint peeling off of them. They looked a day away from collapsing in on themselves.

A fleeting thought swept through my mind and I grinned wickedly.

He can wear a top hat and spearhead the big top, but this was still *my* dream.

I reached up for his hat with no other intention than to irk him when a silk gloved hand swiftly gripped my wrist. Unimpressed gray eyes stared down into my own sky blues. With one of his white gloved fingers, he tapped my wrist condescendingly.

"Tsk, tsk, tsk." Other than a slight turn of his head, he didn't scold me any further and released my wrist. He promptly turned back and continued on.

From the path he was on, it seemed as if we were heading straight on to the big top. He was cutting to the chase, I deducted, intent on something in particular this time. And for him to pass up showcasing his precious, demented home, it meant whatever it was that he was leading me to, it was of importance to him.

"Why not?" I spoke to him for the first time in several months. This dream didn't happen on a schedule. It was an intermittent occurrence with seemingly no trigger. I typically wouldn't mind its reoccurrence if the Ringmaster weren't a part of it and the overall mood of the circus was less dark.

His pace didn't falter although I hadn't continued after him yet. He didn't bother responding to my question. To him, I hadn't spoken. I wasn't there. Ever so the chivalrous individual, wasn't he?

I shrugged and casually walked over to one of the food stands. There were stains of just about every color on the counters, silverware strewn about, empty bottles laying around… I grabbed one and looked back at the Ringmaster who was starting to fade into the fog. It was only a matter of time that he would devise some sort of way to get me moving again.

With another mischievous look on my face, I aimed with my left arm and had my right back ready to throw. I planned on knocking the spectacle of his hat off of his head, but if he kept moving then there was a chance it would hit him instead. Oops? Oh well.

I stepped into the throw and watched as the glass glided silently threw the air bound for its target. Said target spun around in the split second before impact and caught it in an outstretched hand.

I hopped up backwards on the countertop and leaned back against the groaning wood, legs laid out in front of me. He gazed apathetically at my smile and the glass bottle went over his shoulder with a simple flick of his bony wrist. He then removed his top-hat, exposing slicked forward black hair, and held it out for himself to examine.

"A sight to behold, isn't it?" He grinned at his hat and placed it back in position on his head before returning his sights to something less precious to him with a befitting expression.

"Eh, I've seen better." My line of sight raised to the obnoxiously tall silk hat. The ribbon that went around the base was a matching red of his morbid colored topcoat.

His left hand went to his chest and his eyes closed in mock shock, "Wherever?" His eyes opened again to look at me with an accompanying smirk.

"Costume." I shrugged nonchalantly and leaned my head back on the wooden beam, "From the discount Halloween store." I looked at the cloudy sky above us and sighed. Clouds always made me feel more enclosed and I figured they were suiting considering the given situation. The background music emanating from an unknown location changed from the calliope to a melody courtesy of a piano and little bells.

"Huh?" He nodded as if he was considering this. "Fascinating, indeed." He began walking towards me while inspecting the stand I was at with his eyes. He appeared as if he was in deep thought, but his eyes remained blank all the same. They were often unreadable. If you were ever trying to use his body language to figure something out, you weren't going to get anywhere.

"So, what is it this time?" I asked, toying around with a metal rod that had been sticking through the side of the stand. How it got there was just as mystifying as everything else about the whole place. Sometimes, when I was here, I'd forget I was still asleep for the fact that this was so vivid and realistic.

The corner of his mouth curled up, "Oh, you would see, but you seem to have other plans at the moment. And, as you have decided upon acting out, my dear, I have found a newfound fancy of allowing you to make a fool of yourself. After all, it does not waste my time in the slightest."

His hands were closed together behind his back as he passed my stand completely. I had to swing my legs around and sit on the edge in order to properly stare at him confused. The implication was evident in his tone. He spoke up again before I could retort.

"I surely would like to think you did not believe me to be some estranged function of your imagination, but perhaps I regarded your intellect too highly." I could hear the amusement in his voice although I was starting to lose sight of him in the weather. Hesitantly, I got up to follow him. Despite not being remotely as amused as he was. I was still curious of where he was going with this tangent.

As I approached him again, he spun quickly on his heels and faced me. His expression fitted his tone and he smiled fully at me. Wrapping an arm around my shoulders he directed me back the way we'd originally been heading.

"Ah, Miss Estela Nannette Sinclair! I am too complex and simply magnificent to be a mere concept of your thoughts. Really, stop flattering yourself so. It is insulting to me." His pace was brisk and didn't allow me to try to resist without opening a prime opportunity to put me in a headlock. He'd never harmed me before, but I preferred to not take that chance while his arm was so close to my neck. I'd had enough of my fair share of unpleasant physical altercations from my adoptive parents that I didn't need a refresher of the joy it was in my dreams.

It was laughable to even try and consider that this dream I've had for as long as I could remember wasn't just my subconscious mind being quirky. He was just spieling nonsense. That's precisely what dreams tend to be, nonsense. I suppose it wouldn't be surprising he liked to consider himself real.

But, that was impossible. All of it was impossible. Regardless of how different it was from my other dreams, it still had to only be just that. What was the other alternative? An abandoned circus that any sadist or macabre individual would love haunted my head every once in a while when I slept. To what avail? The number of questions arising from that scenario was a many. And for the scenario to be probable, you'd have to reason magic into the loop. Magic.

I shot him a look and laughed, trying not to reveal too much of my bewilderment, "Me flattering myself? I think the over-exaggeration is in you flattering yourself. Really, you're not even real." I grinned matter-of-factly, "But you know? I guess I couldn't fault you too much. I mean, if you weren't your own biggest fan, then who else would be? Who else do you have?" I slid down from his grasp and grabbed a piece of shredded napkin from the littered ground and held it out to him. "But in case I hurt your feelings…"

"How is your family doing, Miss. Sinclair?"

The smooth arrogance of his voice made me an impulse away from socking him in the face. He'd probably just catch my hand, too, like he did with any other projectile.

With a slightly crazed smile on my face, I copied his voice, "I don't know. What about yours?"

His jaw tightened and I knew I finally hit some sort of spot with him. His typically empty eyes darted to me with a deadly glint in them. If he wasn't living in my head rent free, I knew he would've murdered me.

The grin I gave back only made him tense even more, "Ah, pity."

This time when he turned to face me, he did so in a way that I had no choice but to stop from running in to him. His eyes returned to a blank façade, but it was more intimidating than usual. It just about had chills going down my spine.

The seriousness of the situation, though, dissipated, briefly. A yellow-haired clown, whose hair was frizzy like a lion's mane and shoulder length, came and went flying by in a double round-off back handspring. He said nothing. His face was straight. He did his stunt into and out of sight. I tried to suppress my laugh at the unexpected oddity and answer to my earlier question.

The Ringmaster didn't react to the clown in the slightest way. He had to have known what went down behind his back, but he was still focused on me and my remarks. He hit a touchy subject, I hit a touchy subject; it was even. But not in the glorious eyes of this fiend.

"Think, Estela, *think*. I know you have it in you." For a heartbeat his eyes, I believed, tempered but he spun back around and headed off. We were just a few meters from the main tent now. In stride with his attitude, I sighed and followed him one more time.

"Is a show going on?" I asked him. I didn't hear any music or chaos from the inside, but I wasn't sure why we would go to the main tent if there weren't any performances going on.

"No." He answered flatly. I'd have to prod him for more.

"Then, why are we going to the main tent?"

"The Big Top," He corrected me in an annoyed, icy tone to which I rolled my eyes. "We are going to see the kinkers."

For a split second I wasn't going to ask what that was just to relieve him of some stress, but then I remembered who this was and that I cared none whatsoever for his sake.

I grinned, "What's that?"

He turned his head back towards me but said nothing in response. I really didn't know what a kinker was, but he undoubtedly knew I was trying to irritate him further.

As we approached the entrance of the Big Top, the Ringmaster straightened his jacket and whipped a cane out in one fluid motion. The cane was for aesthetics, it never touched the ground unless it was the stage. Not dirt.

His cane was long enough that if he wanted to use it for walking it would reach the floor easily. Near the top of it were two gleaming silver bands positioned right under a simple, black masquerade. He always held the cane right under the two silver bands.

The entrance was open, the worn out and dull flaps tied back. As far as I could tell, there indeed wasn't anything occurring. It was obscure inside. A swift glance from the Ringmaster to the inside brought me to a halt. This naturally resulted in his pause too. He was standing just inside of the Big Top, just where I could partially make him out in the darkness. His face was cold, per usual, and blank. However, I felt like what he was hiding were his feelings of wariness and annoyance. He had to get tired of this at some point. The thought made me relish.

I smiled enthusiastically and clapped my hands together, "The kinkers?" I paused for a moment, smile still in place. "I am going to go out on a limb and guess that that's a nickname for one of your acts. And you know-" I spun around while holding my arms out, motioning to the rest of the circus, "-you have quite the fantastic show going on around here! Very much so in the fact that I do not care to meet any of them. They don't really seem to care for good people; living creatures with hearts, emotions, and feelings, you know? Human beings... Oh, and if you may have forgotten." I then motioned to myself as I began to whisper, "I'm human!"

He tilted his head towards the inside of the Big Top while idly spinning his cane in one hand. The part of his face I could see was contorted into a smirk. Not the vainglorious smirk he usually carried, but a smirk as if I'd struck gold and didn't realize it. It was rich considering there wasn't any gold for me to strike.

Sure, part of my remarks was to bother him because it's the most fun to be had, but it was true that I really did not want to enter a questionable looking, dark vast of space that hosted shows of the inhumane. No, thank you.

"Oh, you do not trust me, dear?" The Ringmaster mocked offense at my statement. He then stepped boldly from the shadows as if he were stepping out onto his stage, his spotlight beaming down from above. Giving his cane another spin he waltzed back to me and leaned down to my face. Even though we were roughly half of a foot apart, nose to nose, my grin still remained intact. I wondered how mad he would be if I'd spit in his face.

"Good." He blinked, "You shouldn't, now should you?"

He chuckled, sounding more sinister, and stood back up, "But what choice do you have?"

I mimicked, a little too easily, his chuckle, "If you force me in there with your freakshow, I will raise chaos inside that tent. What will I have to lose? If I can't choose flight, I'll choose fight."

His face lit up, fascinated at the prospect, and considering all that would entail. The cane spun again.

"Hmm…" He seemed to think this over, the amusement never leaving his face. He looked out and over my head where the rest of the circus resided before looking back down on me. This was sincerely hilarious to him. Seemingly. I blinked and he was back down in my face, looking just a tad bit more serious. That's with sarcasm, may I add.

"By all means, try your luck out, Miss. Sinclair." He chuckled dryly before his voice lowered, "However, you do not want to test their patience, my dear. They are not known for it." He tipped his hat to me before turning back into the shadows of the Big Top and disappeared completely from my sight.

SCENE TWO

"Estela?"

I could feel a hand on my shoulder as I came to.

"Nannette?"

The singsong voice near my ear belonged to one of my best friends, Lement. At best people found him annoying, at worst... He was a very eccentric and mischievous extrovert who could find the fun adventure in any circumstance and knew no stranger. Or at least, that's what it seemed like. Most people could only handle him in small doses, not that the fact bothered him.

I rolled over and buried my face into my pillow, not yet wanting to get up. All that was on my mind was nothing save for the comfort and warmth of my bed.

"You've overslept a half hour, Nannette. This is the last show you'll be able to see and if you don't hurry up, you'll miss out on it; ACT's grand finale."

My mind balked at his words. My eyes shot open as I rolled back over and met his. He was wearing his odd pale-yellow contacts again. They were jarring compared to his light olive skin tone and dark hair. And, they accentuated the ever constant wild gleam in his eyes.

"The circus!" My awareness caught up with reality.

"Ah, there she is. To think, I thought you might've been hungover. It's that pesky underage drinking, Nannette. I tell you it's no good."

"Yeah, sure." I responded, my mind too distracted by getting ready to argue his claim.

"'Yeah, sure.' As in you were drunk, Estela? I'm disappointed!" I could hear Lement feign shock through my closed closet door. A simple peach blouse and navy leggings were the chosen by chance outfit for the day.

"No, it was just oversleeping." I replied as I whisked out of the closet and across the hall to the bathroom, "It was that circus dream again."

Lement and another good friend of mine, Myrtle, were the only two who knew about it. It wasn't anything noteworthy and most conversations didn't broach the subject.

It was a topic that humored Lement, as he enjoyed mocking any remote similarities between myself and the Ringmaster. Not to mention, the dream was a bit quirky and that in of itself was another thing that entertained him.

"Aha, do tell."

"Meh, same old," I brushed through my dusty brunette hair, "Intro, I harassed him, he was unpleasant as ever… It actually seemed short, so I don't know how I overslept."

"Alcohol." Lement grinned jokingly. I contemplated throwing my brush at his head.

"I suppose you would know, good sir." Came my retort. I grabbed a rogue hairband in case I later needed it before whisking away back to my bedroom and grabbing a pair of nude heels from my closet.

"Well, duh."

I grabbed my phone from the nightstand next.

"Are you really wearing heels to the circus?"

Pausing, I shot my zany friend a look, "I'm sorry, are you offended by my heels?"

Lement's chin jutted up indignantly, "And if I am?"

A snort escaped me as I put the shoes on, "Well then, take a heel and shove it."

Lement lit up at the reply he got and laughed heartily as we left my bedroom. Tearing down the spiral staircase, I skipped breakfast and was out the door within a total of maybe ten minutes since Lement had woken me. The fear of being late still prevailed despite that we were now good on time again since I'd opted out of quite a bit of my morning routine. Despite my frantic pace, Lement was right behind me. But of course, he had to have his fair share of fun during my stress.

As I got into his car and closed the door after me, Lement walked along the front of the car in a cartoonish manner. He over animated every movement and bore the most wicked grin on his face to boot. One leg slowly raised into the air and ever so slightly leaned forward until his weight put him down on that leg. The other leg would then repeat.

I rolled the passenger window down and called out, "I should've taken Dulce instead."

His face balled up bitterly at the mention. Dulce was a good friend of both him and I. I'd met the pair, and then some, at my summer job I first started when I was 15. Lement's family owned a traveling carnival that came to town for the summers. Naturally, that explained his playful personality. He was the carnival's jester and our friend, Dulce, was a sideshow performer.

She was an extrovert too, like the both of us, but she was far more laid back and easy going. She wasn't as loud and boisterous as Lement. Regardless of whether I'd mentioned Dulce or Myrtle, any prospect of anyone else taking his role as partner in crime, he'd get touchy. Him knowing Dulce was just an added touch for good measure. Myrtle was a friend from school and not work so mentioning her or any of my other friends probably wouldn't have had as a great an effect.

"Rude." He breathed, finally getting in the car. Retrieving the two tickets from the dashboard, he set them in my lap before backing out of the driveway.

I grinned as I looked them over. Anxiety shifted to excitement. We would make it. We had to; it was the last opportunity.

"I love you and hate you at the same time, Lement."

He chuckled at my comment, "That's my whole charm, Nannette."

I fawned over the circus tickets as we left the neighborhood. The last time I'd seen an ACT show in person was when I was eight. My adoptive parents , Nick and Melissa Sallow, weren't fond of circuses or any other 'abnormal' entertainment. It wasn't *proper* enough… really…

I still kept up with the circus online though. It was likely I knew more about the ins, outs, and every microscopic detail better than the current owners. Speaking of whom, I was bitter about. They were closing the Alexander Circus Troupe after nearly a century of shows. The North American Circus Association had declined to renew their sponsorship of the show.

So, without that additional funding the company that owned ACT had now opted to discontinue the show. The last and largest traditional circus left in the country was getting shuttered. More contemporary circuses were taking over in their place. Contemporary circuses were neat, but traditional ones had an old-time charm to them.

Nevertheless, this would be their last show in Florida on their farewell tour. I wasn't ready for that.

"ACT should've condensed the show, so they don't have to close completely." I mused as I stared at the 'Curtain Call' printed beneath the logo on the ticket.

"Eh, maybe they still don't have the money to or just don't want to." Lement shrugged, "NACA's opening a whole exhibit in their museum with ACT's things so that makes me wonder if they didn't renew their deal so they could capitalize on its legacy for a lower cost."

I thought for a moment, "I hate that's probably likely." My face then contorted into a pout, "That's selfish!"

Lement snorted at my childish whining, "Welcome to modern day Americana, Estela. Home of capitalism and money is king."

Before I could continue sulking, Lement fussed over a driver ahead of us.

"And just to say, why the hell do people drive so slow in the left lane? It's a problem if I ride your ass for not going the speed limit. But you creating traffic a mile long because you won't merge over is fine? I don't understand."

I laughed at his distaste for the minivan in front of us. We were too close to the highway's entrance ramp to try to pass. What a crisis it was for the jokester.

Shaking my head at his complaints, I leaned over and turned the radio on. Obnoxiously loud classical opera music filled the car. I could've sworn I felt a drop of blood escape my ears in protest of the sound.

"Why-" Was all I managed to shout over the music before Lement interrupted, on a new tangent.

"You know, sometimes at intersections; that horse mask I have? I'll keep it in the middle console and then turn this on." He gestured to the radio, "I'll roll all of my windows down, blasting this, and sit there with the mask on and make direct eye contact with the driver next to me."

My voice hitched in my throat as I began giggling at the absurdity.

"One time, someone actually ran the light. They were freaked out."

The giggling broke into light bursts of laughter as he concluded his tale. He was often found doing nonsensical things like this.

"Hey, Lement?"

"What's up?

"What's wrong with you?" I quipped.

He chuckled, "Everything."

* * *

The sight sprawled out ahead from the parking garage top was an entire sea of people. We had arrived within a half hour of show time and mass crowds were still funneling inside. Having been so long since the last time I'd seen ACT in person, it was incredible being back. The energy in the air was filled with excitement. Everyone was here to see the show one last time. The very circus, that is, that kickstarted my love for circus and sideshow related entertainment. My heart fluttered in anticipation.

"Peasants." Lement noted as he looked over the crowds.

"Wow, really, Lement? Coming from you?" I teased.

His snort of amusement was drowned out by the sound of two outdoor merchandise vendors trying to outdo each other. They spiritedly bantered back and forth, laying out their best attempts to lure guests to their respective stands.

"At least I'm not desperately hoarding at the door like cattle. The stadium's not going anywhere." He said matter of fact. "It gives me secondhand embarrassment."

My eyebrow quirked at my chauffer, "If they wait until it clears, they might miss the beginning of the show. Same thing goes with us. Don't be a bear, Lement."

At this, my eccentric chauffer snatched the circus tickets out of my hand and held them in the palm of his hand over the side of the parking garage. My heart leapt at the thought of the wind blowing the two sheets down below into the sea of people. We'd never see them again.

Not having arms long enough to reach them from where I stood, I was forced to be left leaning against the wall and stare at him pleadingly to bring the tickets back to safety.

"Oh, come on!" I pleaded, my eyes darting to the helpless sheets of paper. The rascal only grinned at me. He still kept his palm open, so the tickets had no weight on top to prevent them from drifting away.

"The tickets are going to blow off and we're never going to get them back from people. The arena's sold out." My eyes furrowed together complimenting my anxious smile. I knew he wouldn't intentionally let them fall, but who's to say they wouldn't fall by accident.

"Please!" I continued, hoping it would be sufficient.

He looked off to the side as if he were contemplating my words before deciding that he would cooperate with me. Carefully, he returned the tickets to the safety of the parking garage and handed them over to me.

"Dear child, I hope you've learned your lesson." He scolded, but I was too preoccupied with cradling the tickets to my chest, once again being able to breathe.

"In all seriousness though, you would jump off after those wouldn't you?" Lement asked.

"In all seriousness, yes I would." I answered with a grin.

"Well, that's sad." He laughed before nodding towards the stadium, "But, I suppose since we came all the way out here, we'd better be heading along. Get your popcorn and T-shirts or whatever else you want before the show starts."

A fresh wave of excitement overcame me to be cut short when Lement added, "For your last time." I glared at his back as he walked off for a stairwell, peeved by his laughter at my inevitable unimpressed reaction.

"I'm going to throw you off this parking garage, Lement!" I called to him, begrudgingly following along.

"Ooh, really?" He turned to face me and proceeded to walk backwards, "I'd like to see you try that."

"You'd be surprised."

"Would I now?"

"Just possibly." I stuck my tongue out at him.

The sudden shrill of an alarm blaring momentarily gave me a stroke from the unexpected volume of the car. A quick glance over my shoulder showed that it was Lement's car and a quick glance back at said man showed that it was entirely intentional.

"You scare too easily, Nannette!" He exclaimed, entirely delighted with himself. I set out down the stairwell to join the mayhem ahead.

It bewildered me how they only allocated thirty minutes for attendees to get inside, buy whatever merchandise or food they liked, and get settled into their seats before the show started. I didn't need to be inside just yet to know that all the booths would be packed with people frantic to get their goodies before the show starts. A part of me would pass them up without hesitation. After all, the merchandise was sold on their online store too. But going to a circus and not getting popcorn was unnatural. Inhuman.

I set about getting popcorn from one of the vendors outside before going into the crowd to battle getting inside. At least there would be popcorn to eat while waiting in the inevitable long line.

Only a beat after I secured my place in the concession line, I was met with an elbow to the side. Being the highly ticklish person, I was, I squealed and doubled over before dodging out of the way. As I expected, it was Lement who had caught up.

"I no longer need you, peasant." I straightened back up and dramatically adjusted my clothes as if I were someone cocky, like the Ringmaster… and my adoptive parents…

"You kind of do if you want to get inside without any legal issues." He smiled.

My lips pursed, "You think I'm afraid of legal issues?"

"Nah," he chirped, "And that's the problem."

* * *

It wasn't the sugar of the cotton candy melting in my mouth that had me bouncing in my seat. Though the perfectly buttered and salted popcorn did make my smile even bigger somehow. We were only a few minutes from show time and my eyes were fixed on the countdown clock projected on the show's floor. I was clueless as to how to contain my energy. I felt like a little kid again.

Lement had already teased me about my ecstatic state and was resigned to being preoccupied on his phone since I surpassed the point of coherent and civilized conversation. Every other word was about the circus, being excited, and was accompanied by squeals of delight. Of course, that was ironic because when was Lement capable of civilized and coherent conversation anyways?

My eyes had already memorized the set pieces and rigging equipment's strategic setup, layout, and further details. We were seated in the third row, so we had a perfect view of everything on the main floor. As I gazed at the red curtains the ringmaster would soon emerge from, I wondered what it must look like backstage. Technicians awaiting their cue, performers warmed up and in places, dressers already pulling the wardrobe pieces for the next act, stagehands milling about to triple check that everything was in the right place, and stage managers prepared to see the show run smoothly…

My phone buzzing from where it was tucked safely under the snacks sitting in my lap partially broke my attention. I was too distracted with the spectacle before me that I didn't pay any attention to just who it was that was calling.

"Hello?" My soprano voice had to have been muffled by the lively noise filling the background.

"Estela, you need to come home. We have our lead clientele here you need to meet. Where the hell are you?" The snippy, impatient voice could've only come from one person in particular. My lovely adoptive mother, Melissa.

My full attention was now on the call. Some part of me knew I should've been more concerned and reasonably stressed about where this was headed. But at the moment, my rationality had run away with the circus.

I blinked, "You know I'm-"

"What is all that noise? It's hard to hear you."

A deep sigh escaped me, "I told you I was going downtown with friends. We can't leave yet at the moment. We're at the theater."

I could hear Melissa hiss in annoyance, "Yeah, sure, but where specifically right now? I'll come pick you up. You need to meet them. They run that entertainment company, Parlour Lane."

"Like the amusement parks Parlour Lane?" Melissa ran a creative design company with Nick, but they never mentioned who specifically their clients were and that one of them was that big. But then again, Nick was a man of very few words. He preferred talking with his fists.

Lement's head turned towards me at that, now curious of the conversation.

"Yes, Parlour Lane Parks, Estela. Now where the hell are you?" She huffed. My eyes flicked over to Lement's. The odd colored contacts were still hiding his hazel eyes, but I could see the slight confusion and curiosity.

I quickly put my hand to the phone and leaned closer to talk so Melissa wouldn't hear, "She wants me to come home."

Lement lit up deviously, he didn't need to ask who it was. He just knew.

"Tell her I said hello."

"She's got the people who run Parlour Lane Parks at home, and they want to meet me."

His eyebrows furrowed at that, "Since when did your parents know the Founders?"

I shrugged, "They don't tell me these things."

I put the phone back to my ear, "I can't leave."

The brief silence, I knew, was Melissa trying to keep her composure since there was company over. "You just get up and walk out." She spoke slowly, "I'm picking you up. Which theater?"

I tilted my head back to stare at the arena's ceiling as if it was the source of my current issue. What little composure of the annoyance that had masked my tone was quickly slipping. There was just two minutes left until show. I didn't have time to sit and argue with Melissa. She wasn't going to ruin this moment. My pause only proved to further irk her.

"So help me, Estela. You need to come home. Now! Where? Are? You?"

I scoffed, "I'll be done in an hour and a half or so. Invite them to stay for dinner."

"Excuse me?" She growled, "Do you-"

"Like I don't know." I interrupted, knowing where she was about to go, "I'm going to enjoy this while I have it. Next time have them over when I'm there. Preferably in the next two weeks because I'll be gone after I turn 18."

Lement howled at that with a clap, "And good riddance!' He declared with mirth.

The already steaming Melissa overheard Lement, "Are you with Lemuel again? What have we told you about him…?"

I lowered the phone to hang up, but the ever so impish Lement grabbed it before I could.

"Melissa, doll! I've missed you so much! You should've come with us. But don't worry, I'll bring you back a balloon animal. Tell the Founders I said hello. Hope their amusement parks are going great…" He stopped to listen to the tirade she was probably going on at this point.

Lement beamed the friendliest, most happy smile although she couldn't see it. Further agitating people like this was his favorite hobby when he wasn't blasting classical music whilst wearing a horse mask.

"Oh sure, sure. Ooh, I'll tell you what. I'll talk to you in a little bit. The show's about to start. Love you, queen! Bye." He ended the call with a pleased grin on his face before he turned to me, "I love your mom. Wonderful woman."

An undoubtedly deranged smile took my face, "Oh?"

Lement matched my smile. Cutting the current conversation short, the lights dimmed for the show to begin. And just like that, I was bouncing childishly in my seat again. The band blared and the ringmaster bellowed, "Ladies and gentlemen, children of all ages…"

SCENE THREE

The show itself was far better in person than behind a screen. And although that went for a lot of things, it made it that more disheartening that it was being discontinued. You don't get the same level of awe and anticipation when you're not seeing it in person. There's something about watching people hang from their hair up close that makes it easier to appreciate it.

And it's far more fun in live shows because you can't guess what's next. Circus doesn't always go perfectly, so it keeps you on the edge of your seat. The talent of the performers becomes all that more impressive when their act does go without incident.

There were acrobats, aerialists, clowns, dancers, a human cannonball, cyclists, and stunt performers. It was a grand presentation of colors, flashy lights, jubilant music, and energetic performers. Dazzling costumes, quirky props, and wild acts polished it off. And I'd be remiss to not mention the torrent of confetti at the conclusion.

As the crowds poured out of the arena, someone started a chant. And just like that, the halls leading outside were filled with everyone cheering and chanting on their way out. It was one last hurrah.

Quicker than I'd anticipated, we made it back to Lement's car. There was where the real headache of trying to leave a packed arena set in. It was packed. We were either going to have to wait to back out or just push our way out between the cars.

"What a show!" Lement exclaimed, "Killer finale!"

"Yeah, it was." I agreed, but my agreement was premature.

His voice dropped to a cruelly humorous tone, "But what a shame everyone will forget about it pretty quickly. Another piece of classic Americana bites the dust. Oh, then again, there's that museum. That'd be great if the majority of society regularly visited museums, much less circus museums."

I scoffed, offended on ACT's behalf, "Because the majority of society regularly visits carnivals still? I love 'em, but let's be real. They'd rather go to an amusement park that wasn't taking its rides apart every other month."

Lement's face contorted at that, "Hey?!"

He missed the pointed look on my face as he was too busy backing out in front of someone, cutting them off.

"That's my lively hood, not my forbidden fruit to spite my parents-"

"Rude."

"Just had to go after my personal life. Didn't you, Nannette?" He clutched his chest over his heart dramatically, "You're cold hearted."

A smirk pulled at my lips, "Maybe it's inherited from my real parents."

Lement choked on that with a bewildered grin. We ever so slowly inched through the parking garage. Two more floors until the exit were still before us.

"Aw, come on. Who doesn't love Melissa and Nick?" Lement knew quite well how obnoxious the two were.

Melissa was short tempered. The only time she was in a pleasant mood was before some grand work event or when she was *suggesting* something. It wasn't a suggestion. She was the type of person who was constantly on the phone on account of work, knew what she wanted and got what she wanted, and was very traditional old money. Traditional old money as in you didn't exist if you didn't have some sort of prestigious title. Everything had to be proper with her, orderly and perfect in a nearly obsessive way. And Heaven forbid if I, especially, made the family look bad.

Nick was more kosher generally speaking. Everyone who knew him got along with him. He was just the type of person to speak between the lines. And when that didn't work, then it was the fists. But that was always behind closed doors because he too had appearances to keep.

While Lement knew that they were intolerable, I had never told him about just how ugly it would get at home. It wasn't something I ever talked to anyone about. And considering I had only two weeks left until I was of legal age and could bail, I didn't see the point in doing so now. It would be something I could forget about more easily without having to deal with it anymore.

My only plan so far for when I did turn eighteen wasn't much of one, but it was enough to get out. All the money I made working at Lement's family's carnival just went straight into savings. It was enough money to pay for weekly rates at a hotel while I worked away to get an apartment. It may have not been ideal, but it was far more ideal than staying at home.

In response to Lement's rhetorical question, I shot him a sarcastic smile. My mind shifted to a different line of thought.

"Hey, do you know what a kinker is?"

"You don't, circus nerd?"

"Why do you think I asked?"

Lement chuckled, "An acrobat."

My face balled up amusedly, "How do you get kinker from acrobat?"

We finally pulled out of the parking garage and back to the open roads. Lement tore off as he always did, but I wasn't too eager on getting home anytime soon.

"How am I supposed to know?" Came the reply that was muffled by laughter. "I didn't create the lingo; I just grew up hearing it a time or two. Why do you ask though?"

"The Ringmaster had mentioned something about them." I replied. We were back on the highway now.

"Psh, that old hat again?" Lement jested.

I rolled my eyes, "But I never saw them. It ended just as we were going into the tent."

My phone began buzzing again. Naturally, it was Melissa. And sure enough, she had tried to call multiple times during the show. A series of texts amongst other social app notifications popped up too. I had no doubt that was her as well.

Knowing the inevitable that I would face when I got home, I opted to just leave that inevitability for when I got home. Without a second thought, I rolled the car's window down and promptly chucked my phone out. Lement was caught between a look of bewilderment and intrigue.

"Because silencing the phone is overrated?" Was his quip.

"Because my parents are overrated." The frustration in my voice was directed towards Melissa and not Lement's comment.

"At least it's only two weeks." He lilted.

It was indeed a light at the end of a tunnel, but it was still long enough out that it wouldn't help with whatever was about to go down in the next hour. "Two weeks too long."

In one fluid motion, I sat up, unbuckled myself, unlocked the car door, and grabbed the handle as if I were going to jump out the car as we sped down the highway. Lement swiftly relocked the car doors. I leaned against the door in defeat.

"Geez, Estela, you really are insane!"

"Oh, come on! At least I could spend the next two weeks in the hospital and not have to deal with Melissa and Nick's crap." I said, faking a wistful tone.

"If you jump out the car at this speed, Estela, you'd probably be spending the next two weeks and more in a morgue." Lement pointed out, also pretending to be bewildered by my insincere attempt to jump out of the car.

"Close enough, same results." I noted.

"Nannette!"

"Cecil!"

"Sinclair!"

"Radu!"

"Estela!"

"Lemu-"

Lement's elbow planting itself into my left arm interrupted me and I changed tunes.

"Lement!" I chirped to which said individual shot me a sly grin. It amused me thoroughly that he hated his first name. He didn't particularly care for his middle name either but didn't despise it as much as 'Lemuel.' He felt like it sounded too old.

"Lement, do you hate my name too?" I pondered although I knew that even if he did, he wouldn't admit it.

The slightly confused look that overtook his face humored me.

"You hate your name because you think it sounds old, but my name is an old name too. So, do you hate 'Estela' or 'Nannette,' maybe even 'Sinclair' as well?" I explained.

Lement snorted, "I think your name sounds fine, Nannette. I never really thought about it- well, except for 'Sinclair.' I think with 'Sinclair,' you sound like you're some royal, self-entitled asshole which sounds about right, so it fits."

I jutted my chin up and responded in a pretentious accent, "'...royal, self-entitled asshole...'" Cue eye roll. "Peasant."

"Trash." He retorted.

"Fool."

"Idiot."

"Lement!" I suddenly exclaimed.

He matched my tone, "Estela!"

I smiled at our stupidity.

"Whore." Lement then added causing me to stare at him half incredulously.

"Really?" The question was rhetorical but of course Lement would respond.

"Obviously." He stated seriously before beaming at me innocently and battering his eyelashes.

At the returning thought of the near future, I wished I'd just hopped in a crate backstage at the arena and ran away with the circus.

***

Lement pulled up to the curb since my parents' cars were now in the driveway. A sleek, vintage looking car was parked alongside theirs. I presumed it must have been the Founders. It was a wonder that they had stayed all this time seeing as ACT was a two-hour ordeal. Perhaps they were here for business. Hopefully, they were. If they were there simply on my account, things were going to be a lot worse.

"Thanks, Lement."

"Aw," He drawled, batting his eyelashes dramatically, "You don't have to thank me. I'll be anyone's partner in crime when they have people like that-" His head tilted towards my house, "-to piss off. It's fun!"

I didn't have anything that wasn't remotely moody or cynical to say to that, so I opted to throw him a grimace as I got out. His eyebrow quirked at my lack of response. Typically, I'd follow that up with a jesting remark on the subject of getting into mischief. Seeing ACT with a friend qualifying as mischief was absurd, but it was a tangent I digressed from. Despite Lement's curiosity, he said nothing further.

"See ya." I called over my shoulder as I headed across the lawn. The sound of Lement's car disappearing down the street came no sooner than me reaching the porch. As much as he found irritating people like my adoptive parents funny, he knew for my sake that it'd be best if he wasn't sitting out front when I opened the front door. Founders being there or not, Melissa and Nick would have a meltdown.

As I entered the house, I paused in the foyer. On one hand, it was tempting to just go upstairs and seal myself into my room, blast music, and pretend that Melissa and Nick didn't exist. But they would just wait until I finally did come out and then be even more livid. On the other hand, facing them now with company over could possibly alleviate things. They wouldn't want to make a scene in front of their clientele.

I could hear their voices in the parlor accompanied by unfamiliar ones. The unfamiliar ones sounded like radio talkers back in the 1940s, old fashioned and serious-minded. It wasn't too shocking as the Founders' amusement parks were themed to various eras of yesteryear like the 19th century, roaring 20s, retro 50s… But it was still slightly odd that they were so enamored and dedicated to their affinity for the past that they were talking in vintage accents.

Heels clattering on the tile floor signaled Melissa had heard my entrance.

"Estela?" Her voice was chipper, "Estela, here you are! I want to introduce you to Sir and Lady Founder." Melissa beamed. There wasn't a hint of fury in her brown eyes.

Something I'd always wondered surfaced, "What are their real names?"

Melissa blinked; a pleasant expression still resided on her face, but it looked more fake than it had a second ago. She wasn't impressed. It probably wasn't a courteous question. My capacity to care had checked out upon walking through the front door.

"They're right this way. Come and meet them."

I followed her down the hall to the parlor room. If their vintage accents and 'stage names' weren't enough, everything from their hairstyles down to their shoes looked like they had just skipped from the early 20th century straight to present. They were very classy and polished, but I didn't want to hear Melissa and Nick complain about my passion for my interests being 'too much' when these people's livelihoods were based around theirs.

A friendly smile overtook my face, "Hi!"

Melissa guided me forward since I don't know how to go and shake hands with business elites.

"Hello, Miss Estela. Your parents have praised you time and time again." Sir took my hand to shake. His wife also offered hers and gave a small smile.

"Oh, really? They're too kind." I grinned.

"You have a bright future ahead of you, Miss Sallow."

I couldn't bite my tongue although the smile never left my face, "Sinclair."

A smirk tugged at Sir's lips. "Yes, of course."

I could imagine Melissa and Nick balking internally at my correction. It was just something I couldn't help. There was no way I was ever going to carry their name around. And 'Sinclair' was the one thing I knew of my biological parents. Seeing as I didn't have the same sort of grievance with them as I did the *Sallow's,* I took on their surname as my own. Giving up a child didn't strike me as harsh as manipulating and abusing said child.

"Well, I anticipate we'll be working together in the near future, Miss Sinclair." Sir continued, "It's impressive that you will be taking on your collegiate studies and step into the family business simultaneously, and a *successful* family business at that. We look forward to continuing our companies' collaboration."

A smile and nod were all I had to offer. Melissa spoke up in my place, "As we will always value our partnership. It was Estela's suggestion after all that we reach out to you and of course, the rest is history."

Sir flashed one more smile at me before taking his wife's arm, "It was an excellent decision."

"I'm glad it worked out." I replied.

Melissa and Nick exchanged final pleasantries with the amusement park duo before walking them out to the front. I took the opportunity to drop the formality façade and try to make off for my bedroom. Thirty seconds of meeting two ever so prestigious people wasn't enough of a distraction to make me forget that the consequences of today's adventure were still about to hit. And I still wasn't any more eager to face them.

Unfortunately, I had only made it to the foot of the stairs when Nick stepped back inside. Melissa was still chatting up the Founders on their way out in the driveway.

"Where's your phone?" His voice was flat and empty. The anger was there, but not yet fully unleashed. He closed the front door behind him and motioned for me to head upstairs.

Apprehensively, I turned and headed up the spiral staircase Lement and I had descended just a few hours ago.

"I might've lost it when we were leaving the show."

He snorted, "Really?"

Although he might've known I was lying, that wasn't what would further his anger. It would be the fact that I had wasted nearly a grand's worth of money by losing my phone. That wasn't something I had considered when I was throwing it out of the car. I really just didn't want to acknowledge my adoptive parents' existence at that moment.

"Sinclair."

I hadn't the chance to internally kick myself for that comment too before I'd reached the top of the stairs. The next thing I knew it, Nick pushed me forward as he took a handful of my hair to drag me down the hall to my bedroom. We both knew the startled yelp that escaped my mouth wasn't loud enough to be audible for the Founders to hear outside if they were still there. I was left to somewhat scramble along as he dragged me by my hair. On account of the heels I was wearing, I never caught proper ground to alleviate the weight my hair was bearing.

He flung my bedroom door opened and threw me down on the floor at the side of my bed. Darkly, I grinned knowing the hell that was awaiting me. Two weeks wasn't it? Wasn't that what Lement had said?

"Sinclair?!" He repeated in a roar.

With that he yanked my face back to be greeted by the first of several blows. He once again had a hold of my hair, so he had an opportune angle for reuniting his fist with my face.

"You defied our orders and with Lement of all people?!" He continued in his fit of rage.

He then planted his foot against my ribs and sent me sliding across the floor.

Breathless and blinded by the tears that began streaming down my face, I tried to hold my arms up as a shield. I knew it wouldn't work. Nick had me outmatched in terms of strength. But the reflex to make it stop overpowered that reality.

It hadn't been this bad before. But I guess that was how it always went. The next blowup would be worse than before, but the cycle between he and I never included the 'I'm sorry, makeup' portion that some others had. He was never sorry, and it always got worse.

But two weeks.

Nick grabbed me by the ankle and pulled me back towards him, causing me to whimper. Ignoring my head entirely now, he instead found target in my throat as he pinned me against the wall and began choking me. Now alarmed by my inability to breathe, I desperately tried to pry his hands from my neck. Of course, it was to no avail. As if it weren't bad enough as it was, Nick used to be a wrestler in high school and college. While he hadn't trained in roughly two decades, that influence was still there. And my lungs were currently feeling the effects.

"How do you not see what you're doing to yourself?" He breathed, grip not easing up, "We have everything set up perfectly for you. Your college admission is guaranteed, your career is guaranteed, your future is guaranteed. And you do what? Stand them up for two hours to go see some show with Lement of all people?!"

My head became lightheaded and my vision started to fade. Pain and suffocation became blurred by the total disorientation of beginning to lose consciousness. When it seemed that I would be out within the next second, Nick dropped me onto the floor.

"That psychotic dumbass? He's what, 23, and works at a carnival? He's not going anywhere in life!"

He once again grabbed my head and this time, swung me headfirst into the edge of my nightstand. I could feel my skin split open upon contact.

Miraculously, this was the cherry on top of the lovely sundae. He was finished, physically at least.

"I dare you to see that man again." He hissed over me, I laid on the floor curled in a ball, "I dare you to go wherever the hell you want again when we tell you to come home!"

Nick stomped out of my room, slamming the door shut behind him.

My mind then decided to check out of reality. I didn't blame it. From the repeated blows to my head, one of my eyes was swollen shut. Any coherent thought couldn't properly form, but a sort of instinct made me at least move up onto my bed. It wasn't a minute later that I'd finally lost consciousness.

SCENE FOUR

Upon hearing my bedroom door fling open, I jolted awake, startled. Melissa's brown eyes did not spare me a second glance after the initial assessment of my appearance.

"Get up. You need to be out the door in twenty minutes." She briskly stated before disappearing back into the hallway with a huff.

A bit dazed, I laid on my bed for a moment. My mind still felt out of it from the day before. It didn't feel like I had been out long at all. But sure enough, afternoon had turned to evening, turned to night and then this morning before I woke up.

Blinking my eyes groggily, I slowly sat up. My body protested the movement. It was then when I realized just how much movement involved the neck. I sighed. How was I going to get through a whole day of school? My face balled up at the thought. The temptation to just lie back down and give up was overwhelming, but the natural drive of self-preservation was stronger.

My line of sight rested on the closet door. My legs weren't a victim in yesterday's episode. So aside from the rest of my body's upset, they were steady to stand on. It did take me a moment for my brain to catch up and focus as it felt dizzy now that I was upright.

I brushed that off. As I made my way to my closet, my ribs ached. Apparently a lot of movement also involved that region of the torso. That or they were just sore enough from the foot that kindly implanted itself in them that they just perpetually ached.

Inside my closet, I opted for what would be most comfortable today. A loose fitted tee, hoodie, and shorts fit the bill. I took to the bathroom with my clothes. Nick always left for work far earlier in the morning than Melissa did, so I wouldn't have to worry about seeing his face until later on.

On the way across the hall, Melissa's call from their master bedroom made me freeze in my tracks warily. She emerged a moment later with a folded sheet of paper in her hand.

"Show this to your teacher or whoever if they ask about your face." Was the cold request as she held out the note to me.

I wordlessly took it, mildly surprised that she wasn't going to leave me to have to explain myself to the school. But then again, I suppose I shouldn't have been. Their reputations and lives were on the line if I didn't lie well enough. They couldn't risk me screwing that up.

I moved to continue on to the bathroom, but she grabbed my arm.

"I don't want to hear of you making any allegations." I blinked. "You know damn well we can make anything we need to disappear, disappear."

And anyone, was the clear implication of her words. Still, I said nothing. I had nothing to say to her even if my throat felt up to talking.

I entered the bathroom and flicked on the lights. It was the moment of truth. Stepping into the mirror, I came face to face with myself. The sight of it made my breath hitch in my throat. I looked like I had walked straight out of a nightmare. Perhaps like someone from that circus in my dreams.

The left side of my face was a myriad of deep purples and blues all along my cheekbones and around my eye. It was still swollen enough that my left eye could only open up partially. My upper lip was busted as well, dried blood coating it.

My throat was marked with the imprint of Nick's hand. The magenta colored series of bruises wrapped around either side of my neck.

Then there was my forehead. It too was smeared with dried blood. Unlike my cheekbone, a prominent and ugly knot took up residence just above the bridge of my nose. A gash spanned along the length of the knot. The sight confirmed I looked just as nasty as I felt.

It was a good thing Melissa had written a note. There wasn't any way that I would be able to cover up any of it. Even with foundation, the swelling, busted lip, and gashed knot on my forehead would still be clearly visible.

At the thought, I unfurled the note she gave me. What excuse did she chalk this up as?

A glance revealed she had claimed that I fell down the spiral stairwell. A painful grunt escaped me at that. The stairwell? The knot could probably pass for that. Maybe the cheekbone as well. But the swollen eye likely wouldn't. And as sure as up was not down, no one would think falling down a stairwell caused two bruised handprints on my throat.

I proceeded to clean my face off. Although it wouldn't hide the harsher injuries, I opted to use foundation to change the skin back to a natural tone. With how long I had been unconscious for, I didn't have time to grab an ice pack so pain killers from the cabinet would have to do. I emerged from the bathroom and made my way back to my bedroom.

Grabbing my satchel of school materials, I headed out. Each step down the stairwell surfaced various mental pictures of what happened after the last trek on the stairs. My head still ached, and I was mindful of gripping the railings firmly lest I actually did take a tumble down the metal, spiraled steps. That would be fun.

A cup of water was all that I had in the kitchen. Despite my lack of eating since the circus snacks, my appetite was nonexistent. Placing the emptied glass into the sink, I started my trek to school.

The air outside was a cool temperature. It felt nice in comparison to the hot, humid summer days that were ahead. The sun was cresting the trees and houses, making the sky a beautiful sight to behold. My sensitive head wasn't appreciating it too much, however. I hadn't thought of grabbing sunglasses before I had left the house. Oh well.

The quietness in the neighborhood was nice. I was really exhausted, and the silence was comforting. Once I got to school, I knew silence would be a farfetched concept. Hopefully, I could get a pass to go to the clinic and lie down for a while. I couldn't see any of the faculty objecting to that considering my abhorrent appearance. Despite my soreness, I grinned at the thought of being able to lie down with an ice pack for a while. It wasn't something to look forward to.

Emerging from my neighborhood to the main road, I briskly crossed the street. Part of me did contemplate just laying down on it. Being run over wouldn't have been the worst thing in the world to me.

I made it to my school's entrance. As always, it was lively with countless other teenagers descending upon the building. I was looking forward to it being my final weeks here. I got along with everyone fine, classes were alright, teachers were okay, but it was a chapter of my life that I was ready to end. I wouldn't miss it. And despite the mentioning of the next chapter, and Melissa and Nick's plans for such, I had no idea what was next.

Melissa and Nick were in the mindset that they would simply buy me into their favorite college, and I would step into their company and learn the ropes. They were going to be sorely shocked to find that come my birthday, I would be in the wind. I had no idea of where I was going to go, likely a weekly-rate motel of sorts. But anywhere else would be better than with them. I'd figure things out.

I walked into the halls of Bellgate High. My hood still shielded myself from the glaring lights overhead. The buzz of everyone around me talking to their friends was also starting to make my head spin. It was too much going on all at once for my head to keep up with. It still wanted an ice pack and to go to sleep.

Entering my Government class, I walked back to my seat and rested my head in my arms on the desk. One of my closest friends from school was already in her seat next to mine. Myrtle. She was a petite redhead with the sweetest heart, softest voice, and was mildly naïve at times. She was good hearted and kind of childlike to the point it was funny sometimes.

Having seen my face before I buried it in my arms, Myrtle gasped in horror. As I was sitting to her right side, she had a clear view of the left side of my face. I could practically feel her concerned eyes wander all over my face as she took in the abysmal state it was in.

"Estela?! What happened?" She exclaimed.

My mind felt like it was in a daze trying to follow what she was saying. After a second of processing, my response came in the form of the folded note that had been in my pocket. I slid it over to her before repositioning back to the most comfortable position I could manage at the moment.

Myrtle looked over the note before looking back to me. If she didn't buy the stairwell excuse, she didn't mention it.

"Stela, why don't you go lay in the clinic for a while?" Lightly, Myrtle placed a hand on my shoulder. She was one of the most genuine and caring people I'd ever met. It was refreshing coming from a home spent with the Sallows. For that reason, everyone got along with Myrtle. She was a doll.

Our teacher, Mr. Esparza, walked into the room from the hallway. Once he'd taken attendance, we'd start into our PowerPoint lecture and notes before taking a quiz on last class' notes. Then rinse and repeat. That was every single class. I didn't mind it so much because he was a fun teacher, but the class itself did get a bit monotonous at times.

A shrug was the only reply Myrtle got. It was a valid question. Habit must have been why I still made my way to class instead of the clinic first thing. I sat up and my mind went back to outer space. It would be better if I did go and rested for a little while longer.

"Okay." I nodded. My voice was rough as it hadn't spoken since being strangled.

Myrtle took the note and got up to go to Mr. Esparza's desk where he was submitting the attendance from his computer. My mind zoned back out.

Why was it that I came to school? I didn't feel in the state for it. And if I had seen a doctor, they would probably say to rest and ice my face. That's all I wanted to do. But Melissa and Nick would have a fit if I hadn't come. I sighed.

Myrtle came back to me and tapped on my desk to get my attention.

"Hey, I can take you down to the clinic. He said you can make up the quiz another time. I can give you a copy of today's notes to keep too." She said, grabbing my satchel for me.

I stood and followed her out into the hallway. It was still bright as ever, but the noise had silenced. Myrtle and I were now the only ones in the halls aside from the few late stragglers.

As we walked along, Myrtle sneaked worried glances at me.

"How did your eye happen?" She piped up innocently enough.

I shrugged in response, "I don't know."

One of her red eyebrows raised at that, but she didn't press the issue any further. I could only imagine what she was probably picturing, me falling down the spiral stairwell at home. She was probably trying her hardest to picture how I could've hit my eye specifically like that and depending on how I, theoretically, didn't bust it. I wondered the same thing.

We approached the clinic, but before we went on, a semblance of decency peaked through. Myrtle was a Godsend.

"Thank you for helping me, Myrtle. You're the sweetest." I might've sounded unintentionally detached. My mind had spent the last half hour in some various state of distant and spaced out.

Myrtle gave me a small, but sincere smile. "Of course, Stela. I wish there were more I could do to help." She held the clinic's door open for me and I walked in. Myrtle followed close on my heels and before either of the nurses could say anything, she held the note out to the closest one.

"She's already checked in with her teacher in class and has Gym after this block. I was bringing her here so maybe she could rest for a while." She explained as the one nurse looked over the note.

The nurse nodded in understanding although there was a slight dubious look in her eye. She sure as day didn't believe the excuse but also said nothing for the time being. She guided me back into one of the side rooms while asking a few questions on how I felt and all of where I was hurt.

The knot on my forehead received some ointment and a bandage. The same went for my busted lip. Not having mentioned my throat that my zipped-up hoodie covered, it was still shunned of medical attention.

The moment I had been anticipating the most finally came when she gave me the permission to go ahead and lie down. My brain relished in those words.

I eagerly made my way to a bed and instantly settled myself in. It felt great to lie down again and rest. It wasn't long before sleep enveloped me once more. I readily accepted it.

* * *

It was lunch time.

Myrtle had come back to the clinic to get me before they'd released the rest of the school, so I didn't have to face the masses again.

I still wasn't too hungry, so I ordered a side of fries and a bottle of lemonade. It was the pinnacle, healthy high school meal. But it was at least better than Myrtle's nothing. She always preferred eating before and after school. Thusly it was seldom she ate anything from the cafeteria. I liked to tease her that she was too good for the school's food to which she'd bashfully dismiss, she was too humble to have that sort of mentality.

Once food was acquired, we went to our usual table just outside the cafeteria. It was a nice little courtyard reserved for the seniors to eat at. As we took our seats, the bell rang inside, unleashing the rest of the school.

"Hey, Stela? Do you mind that I already let the others know? I thought it'd be easier for you not having to explain yourself time after time." Myrtle asked as I started into my fries.

I gently shook my head in response, "No, that's fine."

The soreness, aching, and loopy mind only got but so much better in resting. But I was still in decent enough spirits that I figured I would antagonize one of our other friends, Cole. He was a very particular person as things had to be a certain way and stay a certain way or else it would bother him. He was a perfectionist with a dry sense of humor to boot. It was a make or break factor for most people, but we saw past that. Just enough for me to sit in his designated spot to irk him.

I looked beyond the reflection in the windows of the cafeteria to see a sea of bodies milling about. Cole was undoubtedly somewhere lost in the fray, but I anticipated he would be out soon enough. A smirk tugged at my lips. It was the little pleasantries in life to get through tougher times.

My attention shifted to the reflection of the windows as I noticed a third figure nearby that was neither Myrtle nor me. It was too soon for it to have been Cole or the siblings, Rebekah and Aidan. Myrtle's eyes shifted up over my shoulder, shock glossing them.

Before I could turn to see who it was, a party horn unfurled next to my ear. Scaring easily as I always did, I jumped and ducked away from the sound. My ribs weren't appreciative of the quick, sudden movement. My face balled up in response.

"Nannette!" Lement greeted to my surprise, "And Little Red Riding Hood, how charming."

He'd never shown up at my school before, so this was new. I briefly wondered how it would ensue seeing as should the monitors notice someone had just rolled onto property to mingle in with the students, they'd likely call security or police. It wasn't something unbeknownst to him, he probably found the idea more amusing than anything. Rules didn't apply to him in his eyes.

This unpredictable happening only reminded me of what the next unpredictable reaction would be, when he saw my face. As naïve as Myrtle could be and despite the nurses opting to not interrogate me just yet, Lement would see straight through Melissa's lame excused note and be frank on calling that out.

I didn't immediately respond to Lement, but Myrtle did.

"You…" She trailed off, staring- almost glaring at him particularly. My eyebrow quirked up.

"Me!" Lement chirped excitedly as he took a seat to the right of me. Myrtle's odd expression fazed him none whatsoever.

"What are you doing here?" She fussed. She never got testy and bothered by random people before. And Myrtle, Rebekah, Cole, and Aidan had never met Lement before for there to be any sort of terse history.

I could hear the grin in Lement's voice, "Visiting one of my favorite people! It's been *ages* since we last saw each other. And when we did, she threw her phone out my car so I couldn't very well call for a chat."

Myrtle's eyebrows furrowed as her blue eyes shifted to me, "You know him?"

I was now even further confused, and I wondered if there was something I had forgotten seeing how hard I hit my head 'falling down the stairwell.'

"And you threw your phone away?"

"She didn't throw it away, like in the trash. She threw it out, like on the interstate." Lement corrected much to Myrtle's annoyance. She didn't spare him a glance.

"Yeah?" I replied to her first question, my own eyebrows knitted in confusion, "Do you?"

Lement leaned forward, intrigued. He rested his chin on his hands and batted his eyes at Myrtle.

Myrtle's arms were now crossed as she looked on sourly at Lement. She seemed to be holding her tongue like there was a lot she wanted to say but didn't.

"Hmph." She huffed. If I weren't so perplexed and mentally vacant, I would have probably teased her for how childish she looked. But Lement reacted for me, bellowing in mirth at the petite redhead.

"Ooh, are you circus or amusement park?" He inquired. I gave up on trying to figure the two of them out. Fortunately, Rebekah, Cole and Aidan were wandering out for something less confusing for my mind to fixate on.

When Cole did see me and where I was sitting, he stopped. Cool brown eyes met devious blue eyes evenly. He blinked before nodding his head in acceptance and taking the seat across from me.

"Face or not, I will get even with you, Stela." He mused. A taunting grin was the only response that he got to that. He would remember after I'd long forgotten and that's when he'd strike.

I greeted the siblings, Rebekah and Aidan. Both were easy going people unless they were quarreling with themselves in typical, obligatory sibling fashion. Rebekah was younger by a year but was graduating early so she was technically in the same grade level as the rest of us. Aidan focused more so on soccer, already having gotten a scholarship on that account which made me realize soccer was a big enough sport at college that a scholarship for it was a thing. They were getting along today as evident by the fact they were both joining our table.

"We've got a new friend?" Rebekah smiled at Lement's presence.

Aidan was quick to notice Myrtle's lack of enthusiasm, "Who said he's a friend?" He laughed before still offering a hand to Lement in greeting, "Aidan, man."

Lement took it, "Lemuel Cecil Radu in the flesh."

Aidan's hand pulled back quickly in surprise. Lement was wearing a little rogue shock device because he was the type of person to keep assorted party tricks on his person at all time.

"What?!" Aidan's laughter resumed as Lement showed the little gadget on his hand. Rebekah offered her hand out, curious as to what it felt like.

"Really, Lement?" Myrtle chided. As aggravated as she was by his presence, her soft voice didn't sound as menacing as she had probably wished in that moment. Rebekah jumped back with a squeal. Her face was alight in glee.

"Where do you get those?" She inquired. As Lement answered her question and fielded a variety of others on the different types of playthings also to be bought, I focused back on Myrtle.

"You know him?" I asked again. Her glare moved from Lement and back to me where it softened into a sort of apprehension. She fiddled with her fingers.

"Kind of?" She offered hesitantly. "I didn't know you knew him. He's bad company."

I chuckled incredulously, "Now you sound like my parents."

"He really is though!" Myrtle protested adamantly. She opened her mouth to say something else, but whatever it was faltered. A worried glance to Lement and then back to me as it seemed like she was trying to figure out what exactly to say next.

"He doesn't get into any more trouble than I do." I pointed out before taking a swig of lemonade. Lement chimed back into our dialogue.

"Ya sure about that?" He turned to me. His yellow contacts were in again and they immediately noticed the busted lip. His smile dropped into a frown. He turned my chin towards him with a gentle hand and assessed my face. His eyes trailed down to my neck that was covered.

"You're going to hurt her! She fell down the stairs." Myrtle exclaimed.

Lement spared her the most particular look, likely wondering how she believed that I fell down the stairs.

He unzipped the top part of my hoodie and opened the collar area to get a better look at my neck. He was pissed. I said nothing. Cole, Aidan, and Rebekah had been looking on curiously and the latter let out a gasp when she saw the handprints.

"You want to tell me how the hell a stairwell did that, Dollie?" He hissed to Myrtle. The ridiculous jester accent he usually talked in had dropped back to his regular voice. He turned to me, exasperated, and trying to bite his tongue from saying anything harsh in his newfound frustration.

He muttered a series of profanity under his breath as Myrtle sat unsure of how to respond. I remained pretending to not exist despite being the center of attention. Lement stood up and grabbed the little food I had gotten along with my satchel.

"Come on." He sighed. Myrtle stood up too, but furiously.

"You can't take her!" She protested.

Lement turned and leaned over the table towards her, "What? Is she going to stay here? Go back home? Tell me, are you going to hold her hand while her parents choke her out again?"

Myrtle's concerned eyes flicked back to me, "Did they-"

"Do you really need her to spell it out for you?" He shot back. Aidan started to speak up, hoping to calm the situation down so we could probably figure out what to do next, but Lement wasn't having any of it. I had never seen him in any other state but happy, quirky, and weird so this was new to me. But it went without saying his anger was justified.

"Your airstream is already set up for the summer." Lement said to me, lightly pulling my arm to lead me away, "You can just stay their indefinitely. You don't have to work to keep it like summer stock, it's yours."

I turned to look over my shoulder back at my friends who were watching on in various states of shock and concern. Myrtle still looked distraught that I was leaving with Lement. What was their history? I figured I'd ask later on.

Lement guided me to where his car was parked in the student parking lot. One of the monitors noticed our exit and started moving towards us, calling for us to stop.

Everything was still pretty disorienting and surreal enough that I just watched them as Lement opened the passenger door for me and I got inside. Said friend just ignored them completely and walked around to the driver's side. The monitor started jogging over but didn't have a chance as Lement zipped out of the spot and the lot. We were bound for his family's carnival, The Midway.

SCENE FIVE

We drove through the gigantic metal pillars that held the curved beam cheerfully announcing 'The Midway' in flashing neon lights. It was as conspicuous and noisy as the carnival itself. Bold colors, bright lights, loud music, and the distinct smell of too much sugar, butter, and oil filled the air. Simultaneously, it was both exhilarating and exhausting.

And in the craziest turn of events, Lement became mute. At least, he was for the entire car ride here. Undoubtedly, he was stewing over my less than stellar appearance. His teeth had to be grating away with how tightly his jaw was clenched and his grip on the steering wheel had turned his knuckles white long ago.

He took the back path that was long worn from the countless cars that came before us, unceremoniously wearing the grass down steadily to bare Earth. It was pretty brief considering the location of the backstage area. It was the only section of this field that had enough space for the silver sea of airstreams.

Needless to say, the carnies lived in an airstream park. This included the summer stock who got their own rentals for the duration of their employment.

All of the airstreams varied in sizes, respective to who all was living in that particular airstream. They were lovely little capsules from another era, perfect for forgetting the modern world.

The car screeched to a stop just behind one of the gates that led to the carnival's midway. I'd been through it numerous times before, typically in full costume for the parade or bound for working the Ferris wheel. How the circumstances had changed. At least the carnival didn't open for another hour or so.

Wordlessly, we got out of the car and started down the midway. I wasn't all too sure of where in particular we were going. I had expected to end up in either of our airstreams and finally confront the situation head on. My momentary willpower to ask where we were going didn't exist.

We came right up to the Fortune Teller's tent at the front of the midway. It was a swirl of deep shades of purple with gold trimming. The sign out front read 'Your Future Awaits.' Painted on the front side of the tent were giant tarot card characters. The irony was not lost on me that I didn't need a tarot card to tell me how bleak my future was. My dark sense of humor was doing well enough to make me snort in amusement at myself.

Lement pulled an entry flap aside, "Come along, dearie. Annie doll will take care of you."

His voice had reverted back to the odd, jester character accent although it was clearly forced. He seemed to struggle with his composure and thusly had a wild gleam in his eyes.

A small smile was my only response as I ducked into the tent.

Annie was Lement's mother. For whatever reason, he called his parents by their names, Louis and Annie, rather than the traditional, dad and mom. To boot, he was typically curt with them. Friendly, but curt. As in the, 'Thanks, mom. Now bye!' before skipping off to whatever trouble he'd get himself into. His parents didn't pay him any mind.

Inside, the unhealthy scents of the carnival were replaced by lavender and incense. I was pretty sure since day one that Lement's family carnival was where the stereotypes and clichés originated from.

The number of candles lit combined with the incense, strings of beads and lights, tarot cards at the entrance, so forth and so on created the typical mysterious feel. The thing was, though, this wasn't all just for show. This was genuinely Annie's lifestyle.

Lement disappeared into the backroom where Annie did her reads. I remained in the lounge area fidgeting while assessing just how long before one of the candles would light the silk drapes overhead ablaze. The sound of Annie's singsong voice filled the silence.

"Stela?" Annie came bustling out of the back with a look of concern adorning her face. It contrasted her typically cheerful demeanor and twinkling laughter. She was who Lement got his zaniness from.

Her long, flowy skirt that matched the color of her auburn hair swished jarringly as she rushed to clasp her hands on either side of my face.

"What animal did this to you?" Small, delicate hands flittered over my face, turning it this way and that, "… oh, dear. Come. I have just the thing for you."

She whisked me away to her backroom and sat me down on a small sofa.

To be honest, I expected her to pull out essential oils, crystals, and herbal teas. It wasn't necessarily a conscientious thought more so just a general expectation like expecting lightning in a thunderstorm. So as such, I was too surprised and mildly disappointed when I saw a simple first aid kit complete with band-aids, methylated spirit, morphine, and cotton. She tore off a piece of cotton and dabbed a bit of the methylated spirit on it.

"This will sting a bit. Sorry, love." She crooned, leaning over me.

Nothing could've hurt as much as the actual incident itself, so I just shrugged. She gently pressed the cotton swab against my lip before moving up to my eyes. The latter of which, I was certain had just morphed into an indiscernible ball of purple. That likely wouldn't be going anywhere anytime soon.

"Don't worry, child. It'll clear up soon, okay?"

Despite the mild, but steady pain that befuddled my mind, I still chuckled to myself at Annie's assurance that was perfectly timed with my thoughts. But 'there is no such thing as coincidence' I could hear the Ringmaster say in one of my past dreams, 'merely purpose. Do not be deceived.' I internally rolled my eyes.

"Now, what is today's date?"

"June 13th." I responded.

"What's your name?"

"Estela Sinclair."

"And where are you?"

"The Midway."

"Hmmm." Annie nodded as she gazed at me with her arms crossed. I supposed I passed the concussion test.

Being the co-owner of the carnival, I was confident that Annie had seen her fair share of broken bones, bumped heads, and bruises. Experience cultivated her prowess.

"Lift your shirt." She instructed with the air of a medic.

Obediently, I lifted the tee and jacket. I searched her face for alarm, but it instead remained expressionless. Her hands against my skin were cold as she felt along my ribs. I bit back a gasp of pain when she touched a particular sore spot under my bottom right rib. She then stood back up; lips pursed. I was prepared for her pronouncement.

"You don't seem to have a concussion and luckily, your ribs seem to be only bruises. In a few days, you should feel all better. But for now, take this-" She stooped and lifted an orange pill bottle and popped out a pill, "this should help with the pain."

"Thank you." My response was raspy. I dry-swallowed the pill as I wondered where Lement had disappeared to. On the subject of disappearing, Annie stepped out momentarily to return with a steaming bowl and bread.

"Eat this and rest, alright?" She insisted. I nodded my head in agreement. I'd forgotten how little I'd eaten today until the smell of the soup hit my nose.

I wasted no time in putting the spoon to use. My stomach was the happiest it'd been since before Nick bashed it in. It was like a kid in a candy store; broth, meat, and warm bread... for as unhealthy the concession foods were, the employee food was high end. As in dinners would be roasts, potatoes, veggies, and soufflé or chicken parmesan, cannelloni, breadstick, and tiramisu. The cooks *spoiled* the carnies.

Soon, the bowl was empty, and I set it down at the foot of the sofa. My eyelids were droopy as if I hadn't spent enough of the day unconscious. I reclined back, intent on letting the food settle for a minute before setting off to find Lement. Just a minute.

* * *

My eyes fluttered open to see my school bag laying on the bed next to me and my jacket on the bed post next to it. A lone, warm glowing lamp was the only lighting in the room. It wasn't lost to me that I was now in a bed and not Annie's sofa. The scent of lavender and incense was replaced by subtle cologne. The soft brown comforter I'd seen before told me just where I was.

Here I had anticipated two things. One, not falling asleep outright. Two, having to find Lement. Lement found me.

It was as I slid out of his bed that it dawned on me that I could see clearly out of my swollen eye and my ribs weren't aching anymore. Tentatively, I prodded at my ribs, fully expecting to immediately regret it. Peculiarly enough, I didn't.

My hand then traced my lips. They were fine. I felt my eye. It was normal.

My eyebrows furrowed.

An incredulous snort escaped me, "How long was I asleep?" I wondered aloud to myself.

I felt over my injuries again and gazed at them unsure of what to make of their quick disappearance. Maybe I shouldn't look a gift horse in the mouth. But still…?

A knock at the door pulled me from my head.

"Nannette, you decent?" It was Lement.

"Was I not decent before?"

"When are you ever?" His mood had improved in the duration of my nap it seemed.

My chin jutted up and I crossed my arms like he could actually see my reaction, "Since when is it appropriate for a 23-year-old man to throw a 17-year-old girl into his bed?"

I could hear Lement cackle in response, "Since it's legal in the state of Florida."

I swung the door open to see Lement leaning against the kitchenette counter. His pale-yellow contacts weren't in anymore, exposing the hazel eyes he also got from his mother. They were casually amused by the current banter.

"Oh, so at 17 I can date whoever then and its legal?"

One of his eyebrows quirked as he mulled that over, "Maybe? That's a Kellan question."

The Terrifying Triplets were a thing in the Midway. They consisted of Lement and Irish twins Briley and Kellan, who were two Jacks. The brothers were in the sideshow troupe that was a multi-talented 'jacks of all trades' show; meaning they sword swallowed, fire breathed, threw knives, suspended themselves from piercings alone, and so forth.

Briley, aka Trickster, was the wild, aloof brother who some time seemed to have a screw loose as he'd sit by himself and laugh for literally hours on end. Kellan, aka Mayhem, was the pessimist, spiteful, utterly horrid to be around twin. He stayed in a perpetually ill mood and enjoyed either pissing people off or upsetting them.

"Pass on Kellan. I was asking for Dulce." I grinned knowing the jester's inevitable reaction.

His eyes couldn't have rolled further back into his head, "Ewww, de Leche's too old."

I had opened my mouth to retort, but Lement had already shifted topics.

"Annie did a perfect job on you." He mused, hooking a finger under my jaw and examining my face.

"Yeah, what was in that soup?" I inquired.

Lement then proceeded to make the biggest show of mock wondering. His finger went to his own chin and his eyes lit up wildly as he looked around for good measure. He started to say something just to scoff, feigning perplex. His hands then went to his hips as he shook his head.

"You know…" He bit his bottom lip, "Food, maybe?"

An unimpressed deadpan was the only response Lement got.

"How do you and Myrtle know each other?" Lement's eyebrow shot up peculiarly as the tables turned to me shifting the topic. A wry smirk decorated his face.

He shrugged, "Family history…"

"Can't relate." I quipped darkly, "Do tell."

"Later," He replied, dropping the character accent. His expression was fairly neutral, but there lacked the hints of mischief that seldom, *seldom* left his face. It was easy to forget that he had to have real feelings somewhere inside even though they were barricaded by his wild personality.

"There's something I want to show you." And just like that, the mischief was back.

I couldn't help but return the wicked grin he had on his face. He gestured me to follow him before skipping out of his airstream's door.

Outside, the sun was just beginning to peak out of the horizon. Most of the rides that I could see were still awaiting their riders. Considering the time it was when I dozed off, it was a wonder to me that the carnival wasn't open yet.

As I sped up to catch the excited jester, I called ahead to him, "What time is it?"

He came to a halt outside of my airstream door, "Too early." He dramatically huffed.

"But it was morning, almost midday when I fell asleep."

His face lit up, "That was yesterday, Nannette."

My face crumpled in skepticism immediately, and my arms crossed my chest, "I was not asleep for that long." I protested adamantly. I was sure that my body might have been tired considering what it had gone through, but I had still slept so much since the incident that there was no way that I'd slept for a whole day straight.

"Yes, you were." He chirped, matter of fact, before opening my airstream. The white curtains that framed the doorway inside billowed out, beckoning me to go inside.

I didn't believe what Lement was saying for a hot second, because he would be the type of person to make that up with the sole intention of messing with me.

I rolled my eyes and went to enter my gleaming abode, "Oh, it's my airstream." I said in mock shock, "I'd never seen it before. Thanks for showing me."

Lement unceremoniously pushed me aside into the dining booth on the right. Fluffy dark green and purple cushions greeted me as I glared back at my friend. He bore the most innocent smile and batted his eyelashes.

"Look!" He stepped aside to reveal the rest of my airstream behind him. Everything from my bedroom at home was now relocated and decorating the living space. He'd managed to get into the house, pack all of my things, and bring them over here without Melissa or Nick knowing… just yet. A new phone was on the counter top as well.

Maybe I had slept for a whole day. There was no way Lement would've been able to do all of that in the time between me falling asleep and waking up if it was still the same morning. My mind had to take another second to properly process what I was seeing.

I hurled myself into Lement, meeting pure muscle that was the only saving grace for us not crashing to the ground. He was zany, over the top, passionately wild; but he was also a truly good soul underneath. Although he spent most of his time being a pissant, he was more than capable of being an endearing, kind person when he wanted to be. This carnival gave me my favorite people.

"How'd you do that?"

I felt him smile against the top of my head, "A magician never reveals his secrets."

"You're a jester, not a magician."

"Well, I want to be both!" He childishly protested, ruffling my hair for good measure. "Besides, doing the impossible is part of my job description, peasant."

I paid no mind to his newfound aspirations and instead brushed past him to mull over my belongings. Considering it was a new day, it was about time to freshen up. Just a quick shower and it'd be as if the water had washed the past two days away. I was more than eager to get to the part where I pretended they never happened and now focus on what's ahead… and enjoy the fact that I was finally free of Melissa and Nick.

For the past fourteen years of my life, I'd been counting down the days until my eighteenth birthday. Right on the day of, I'd be out. I was fully prepared for that battle of getting out of the house. My adoptive parents wouldn't care that I was legally an adult. They owned me, not for raising me, but because I now am a reflection of them. They'd lose their minds if I made our family look bad.

I'd never really given much thought on what I would do after I left home. What's the point of figuring out what you're going to do next if next ends up not happening? The goal was just getting out. From there, I knew I'd make use of my summer stock savings and go to school or work as I got a clearer picture in mind. But I never fully dwelled on it.

Speaking of school, I was probably late.

"Well, I'm about to become undecent, so shoo." I said, pulling out clothes and toiletries from my old suitcase. It made me chuckle to think of just all the nooks and crannies Lement got in to *relocate* my things and some of what he thought were my things. This suitcase was up in the attic space above my closet. He had done a clean sweep of the lot.

"It's *in*decent, not 'un.'" Lement clasped his hands together, bearing a ridiculous smile.

"Can you tell me what the proper grammar for telling someone to 'piss off' is?" I shot back.

Lement strolled to my door before looking back at me with his chin jutted up, "Piss-eth off-eth."

I beamed at him sarcastically, "Heed those words."

As Lement opened the front door, he did one theatrical bow before saluting me with his middle finger and exiting my airstream with a cackle.

* * *

The pathways that flowed from one airstream to the next were lined with posts. Strings of dim, amber colored lights zig zagged overhead of the paths, connecting one post to the next. While the bulbs weren't lit during the day, at night the glow that reflected off of the shiny, silver airstreams was a lovely sight.

No sooner than I got to Lement's airstream, the door flung upon. He stepped out, wavy jet black hair slicked back and carrying a pale-yellow jacket on his arm. For whatever reason, he'd dressed up into grey slacks, a white button down, and black suspenders. It wasn't atypical for Lement to spontaneously wear outfits that were out of place for essentially no reason.

"Feeling dapper?" I asked him as he locked his airstream's door.

He turned, swirling the ring of keys on his finger before placing his hand in a pocket, looking thoughtful, "Snazzy." He corrected before eyeing my satchel. "The hell you still have that for?"

"You're either going to play chauffer or get mugged," I replied, pointedly gesturing to the pocket he had stuck his keys in.

Lement's contacts-free eyes lit up, taking my statement as a challenge. After going on three years of knowing him, I should've known this would become another game to him. He then proceeded to take the key ring back out and dangle them just above me.

"You need these, Nannette?"

"I need to get to school."

His face immediately balked at that, "Ew?"

"Yup, ew. Get to stepping, toots. I'm about to graduate."

A commotion ahead, further into the sea of airstreams, interrupted us. The clashing sounds of pots and pans rang out over top of the racket of an excited crowd roaring with laughter. A lone, comically sad sounding clown horn hooted. A few shrilly, startled screams followed suit. It sounded like mischief. I liked mischief.

Lement's expression of amused pity, like I was missing out on something or not connecting a line of dots, drew my attention from the previous curiosity that briefly encapsulated me.

"Okay. I'll have Dulce take me."

So, Dulce was a mutual friend of ours. She was part of the same sideshow troupe as Kellan and Briley. An old soul, if the '70s, sultry bohemian hippie flower child manifested as one singular person then it was her. I'd never known a more easy-going person who had a passion for referring to everyone by endearments. But Lement never failed to get triggered by her.

She was an older sister figure who knew just the right buttons to make Lement sensitive. It was like the saying went, it's not what you could dish but what you could take. Lement liked dishing, but not taking. He liked making the joke not being the joke. Enter Dulce.

As such, I loved pulling the Dulce card. He didn't like the prospect of her one upping him.

Lement grimaced, "Okay, have Dulce take you." He waved me off dismissively, "But Dulce and I won't be able to help you when your parents and the police show up there to take you home. And there, you won't have a choice. You'll be going home with Melissa and Nick who will be upset that word got out of what they'd done, that you ditched school, and you came to live here. Dulce and I won't be able to help you if you're dead."

My jaw clenched at Lement's candor. The fact that he was right didn't help any.

"Now here, we can make you disappear like you never existed. How will they find you then?" He batted his lashes with a grin. When I didn't immediately respond, he leaned forward and cupped his ear. It was a gloating taunt for me to question him.

"You underestimate my contentedness with being dead." I deadpanned. I didn't let him see the amusement I felt as an unimpressed countenance overtook his face.

"My sister happened to say something similar before she was killed." With that, he turned to head towards the commotion still going on. Seemingly indifferent to his own words, he strutted along while leaving me stunned.

Effectively, my previous humor was gone in the unexpected turn of events. But I wondered if he was even being serious or laying his own dark sense of wit on me. He'd never mentioned having any other siblings aside from his younger brother Dennis. His family have never acknowledged the subject either, not that they were obligated to. But for as long as I'd known them and worked at the carnival, it was a wonder *someone* hadn't slipped up once if it was true.

"What?!" The question escaped me in a sort of confused, exasperated laugh.

"You're going to miss out on the fun, Nannette!" Lement called cheerily over his shoulder, still continuing onwards.

I rolled my eyes.

SCENE SIX

The Jacks & Jackettes were at war with the clowns again. The latter of the two saw it fit to ransack the former's green room.

In the middle of the myriad of airstreams was the Rounds, a hub of green rooms for every troupe and employee department in the carnival. While each had their own dedicated green room, each was open to anyone regardless of what department or troupe they were in.

The green rooms were lounges at the heart of the carnival's backstage operations and featured something precious around these parts, air conditioning. The dressing rooms and employee tents located near the carnival venues did not have that.

For the first time, I wasn't throwing myself headfirst into the mix of the chaos, inciting, or instigating. I was still caught up in Lement's remark. Said fool *was* in the mix of the chaos, inciting, and instigating. My face remained frowned.

My eyes darted over the sight before me. The clowns had strewn every bit of furniture, décor, lighting, curtain, mirror, literally everything from the Jacks & Jackettes' green room all about the outdoor entertainment area that separated the two.

A clown was chasing a Jackette around with cans of spray paint mixed with fart spray and confetti. A Jackette had pinned a clown to the ground with stakes and throwing knives. As such, that clown was getting trampled by everyone else. One of the Jacks, namely Briley, was perched atop the clowns' green room, in the process of leveling it with a chainsaw. I knew where his brother would be.

I made my way behind the Jacks & Jackettes' green room to where the outdoor picnic table was set back in its rightful place and Kellan sitting there smoking, listening to the noise on the other side of the tent.

I took my spot next to him on the bench, straddling it so I can quietly stare at him until he got annoyed enough to acknowledge me. If I'd just struck up conversation, there was a good odd of him flat out ignoring me unless what I'd said piqued his interest enough. My newfound method of pissing him off first meant that he'd concede just to get me to shoo faster.

"What?" The attitude in his voice sounded more like exhaustion.

"Did Lement really have a sister who was killed?"

Evidently, I didn't need to stare him down for his attention as this subject was something that interested him enough.

"Mildred." He breathed smoke; the corner of his mouth turned up. He tilted his head back to the sky with a smile before turning to look at me. "What do you care?"

"I don't know. Maybe I care about one of my best friends? One of your best friends." I retorted, unappreciative of his callousness.

"If you care about him, then leave it alone." He huffed, "You're just finding out? Does it not click that he doesn't like to talk about it?" The twin pointed out.

I could understand where he was coming from. His line of thought was valid and something I'd respect. But initially, I had been unsure, still, of whether Lement was joking or not. Maybe not everyone would joke about something like that. Everyone except me.

"Got it. You want to now explain to me why you'd know the legalities of a 17-year-old and a 23-year-old being together?"

Briley's manic laughter could be heard over what sounded like the collapse of the clowns' green room.

Kellan took another draw of his cigarette. "I like to know just exactly what laws I'm breaking."

"You're sick."

"At what point does a five-year age gap draw concern? At what level of risk does it constitute reckless endangerment?"

With a huff, I rose from my seat to leave Kellan to being Kellan. I wasn't surprised that he had a disturbing knowledge of legalities on questionable subjects, but I still wasn't any less tolerant of it.

"I'm not sorry," He continued, flicking his eyes up to me with a glint in them that never bode any good, "You want to ask someone about Lement's sister? Why don't you ask your nonexistent father?"

I snorted and grinned at him, "He's too busy bedding the corpse of your mother."

Kellan's face scowled at that, but he said nothing. He simply returned to his smoke.

Back tracking to where the carnival brawl was dying with the clowns' green room, I glanced over the disheveled mess lying about until I found the mini fridge face up next to the fire pit. That mini fridge always held a surplus of one thing.

"Babe, grab a stout. The IPA is only in there because Kellan hates himself." Dulce's voice called from where she was crouched atop her troupe's green room. She had one of the clowns, Daisy, hanging from body suspension hooks by her clothes.

I heeded her advice and grabbed an extra to toss up to her, "You want to steal some of the clowns' hair dye and dye my hair?"

"Color?"

"Mauve."

"Yes." She smiled and flicked her dark indigo hair behind her shoulder before doing a front roll down off of the green room's roof. "Finally." She added.

It'd been since the dawn of time that I wanted to dye my hair. But for so long as I wanted to draw breath living under my parents' roof, it wasn't happening. And if I couldn't graduate anymore, I at least could dye my hair.

“You’re my favorite.” I beamed, my own way of saying thank you.

“I know. I’ve always known.”

* * *

“Dove, I wish you’d moved in sooner.” Dulce was playing with my hair at this point, having finished dyeing it. She was now enjoying her latest masterpiece.

I raised my bottle to her in agreement before topping it off, “I need another stout.”

Dulce paused playing in my hair long enough to lean over my shoulder, “Drink one for me. I’ve got double side.”

“Copy that.” I replied, hopping out of the chair to eye my new color closer up in the mirror.

Seeing as the clowns had disheveled the Jacks & Jackettes’ green room, we resolved to dyeing my hair in their dressing room instead. The room was lined with rich, red curtains. Strings of lights lined the top of each, casting a cozy glow inside the space.

Along three of the walls were a series of makeup mirrors and chairs. The vanities at each were littered with foundations, eyeliners, stage blood, glitter, hair pieces, and some of the smaller costume pieces. The fourth wall was where all the costumes resided.

They were a collection of velvets and satins, sequins and leathers. The costumes for the day were all that were here, as the costumes team sent batches in and out at the top of every day according to what acts were going to be put on.

Dulce had plopped me down in her makeup chair and went to work. We hosed the dye out afterwards outside in the grass. By that point, the sounds of games, midway music, and running rides signaled that the carnival had opened.

With a smile, I turned back to Dulce, "Thank you!" I drawled.

In response, she blew a kiss before turning to their costume racks, "Get Briley for me?"

"On it."

I ducked out of their green room and followed the dirt path around the back half of the carnival. The layout of it was a simple circle with the midway cutting straight down the center. The sideshows and rides were along the circle's edge and the concessions, games, magician's parlor, and fortune teller booth streamlined down the midway itself.

What activity there was around the airstreams and the Rounds now consisted of performers and employees bussing about regarding their day's work. Everyone caught up in the earlier shenanigans had since dispersed, save for Briley and Daisy, who was fussing at the former from where she was still pinned by suspension hooks. Briley remained dedicated to the cause of vandalizing the clowns' green room, currently decorating its remains with graffiti. It'd been a solid two hours since the showdown had kicked off.

I made my way to the Jacks & Jackettes' green room where they had brought all of their belongings back inside but hadn't the chance to set it all back up as it was. I grabbed another beer out of their mini fridge.

Heading back to their green room's doorway, I took my empty bottle and beamed it at the Jack's head.

His surprised cry was complimented with the hanging clown's laughter.

"Double side, dumbass." I opened my new bottle and took a swig as Briley spun back on me.

Without warning, the empty bottle soared back to me and cracked against the bottle at my lips. With a slew of profanities, I choked on the stout.

My glare shifted to the redhead before me who remained crouched with the most mischievous grin. He briefly snickered before tearing off to, presumably, their dressing room. My scowl followed him until he disappeared out of sight.

"You want to get me down now?" Daisy spoke up from just above me.

I turned to meet her gaze with an eyebrow raised. I looked over her predicament and smiled, "Nah."

I set off back to where Briley had disappeared to, leaving Daisy protesting atop the green room she had earlier disemboweled. It was always fun to watch the double sides, each one was never a repeat of another.

The double sides were typically done between three or less troupe mates. The sideshows were done in their respective venue by the whole troupe. The double sides were like a sideshow of the sideshow. In between sets, some of the troupe members would go out on the midway and do a brief little show for fun.

My pocket vibrated. Pulling my phone out to see the cause, I found that it was on account of another redhead.

"Hey, Myrtle." I answered.

The degree of exasperation I was met with somehow managed to surprise me.

"Where are you? Are you okay?" Even in her despair, her voice still sounded child-like and melodious.

"I'm fine. I'm still at the carnival. Actually, doing better than I was before-"

"I told you Lement's bad news. Are you going to go back home? You can stay with me."

My eyebrows crumpled; I'd never known Myrtle to be this ill before. She was always sweet, bordering shy and the most easy-going person I'd met. That reminded me of another point I was curious about.

"I'm two beers in, living at a carnival, Myrtle. I'm living my best life." I joked though I knew she wouldn't be impressed, "So, what family history do you and Lement have?"

There was a pause on the other line. I could tell that whatever it was, was a point of contention. That only piqued my interest more.

"Are you childhood friends? Exes?" I continued; the humor clearly laced in my voice. For every person to decry Lement as being some abhorrent individual for his eccentric nature, I enjoyed being around him all the more. If anything, to piss them off.

Myrtle, however, I wasn't intending to upset. I knew she was genuinely concerned for my wellbeing. And with the two's stark contrasting personalities, it wasn't but so much of a surprise that she didn't like him.

"No!" Myrtle vehemently denied, causing me to chuckle.

By this point, I'd stepped out into the carnival. It was busy enough. It usually wasn't until later in the day that the bulk of the crowds would swarm in. There was still enough activity to bring life to the funfair yet.

"He's a terrible person, Estela. He's mean, cruel-"

"I've known him for three years, Myrtle. He's never been so much as angry before around me until my parents choked me out. And I'm not saying that there's not a side of him that I might not know, but there's definitely a side of him that you haven't known yet." I interjected.

Myrtle fell silent again before piping back up, "Three years?"

"Yes?"

Myrtle sighed, "Estela, that side that he's shown you isn't real. Once, before his sister died, it was. But ever since, he's horrible to people, he uses people. I didn't know that he's been around you all this time. You need to come stay with me."

It was my turn to go quiet. Here I was just finding out that Lement had had a sister, that Lement and Myrtle knew each other, and now Myrtle was relaying her unpleasant experience with him. I didn't disbelieve it, but I still felt that there was a wrong context, or she might've been mistaken.

I whole heartedly trusted her and I whole heartedly trusted Lement. I didn't know what to say regarding their history.

"I'll see you soon," I assured Myrtle, "I'm here until I turn eighteen and can legally be on my own, but I'm not going home, and I can't go back to school."

As I made a right to head down the half circle path the Jacks & Jackettes venue resided, I could hear the applause and excitement of people up ahead. Briley and Dulce were already out.

"Estela, you can't stay there." Myrtle was adamantly pleading.

A part of me knew that I was going to eat my words, that there was a strong potential that I would learn the hard way. It was a miniscule part of me that wasn't backed by any sort of rationality, as my rationality defended Lement. I cared about him, about Dulce, everyone, and the life I had here at the carnival from the three years that I've worked. I was prepared to eat my words, I was hungry.

"I've been here for three years with no indication that I shouldn't trust any of my friends here. They're like family and they're a better family than the one I was supposed to have. I'll talk to you later, Myrtle. I'm fine."

With that, I reluctantly hung up on her. It hurt, but I didn't want to hear any more of it. The stresses caused by my adoptive family were plenty for me to deal with at the time being. Despite my unhealthy curiosity, I didn't need any other issues piled on.

As I made my way towards the double side, I let the energy of the carnival distract me.

John Lance was an operations manager, tasked with delegating the day's chores and overseeing them. He answered to Lement's dad, Louis, only. And as such, he was an aristocrat conducting the affairs of the front-line workers from a high horse. He was currently barking at the carousel's operators for not properly fussing at the kids running amok.

The attraction was temporarily down long enough for a maintenance worker to check over the gears, motors, crankshafts, and sweeps. It was likely a double check before the day got further under way. The kids in line were entertaining themselves in the meanwhile by making a jungle gym of the rails.

Disregarding the scene, the collective scent of fried dough, caramel apple, and pizza reminded me of the unhealthy diet ahead. While the cooks in the pie hall backstage often prepared far healthier meals than the carnival itself did, it was too hard resisting a funnel cake. I now had to have one.

Despite the temptation, I settled into the crowds around Dulce and Briley. They were excitedly egging the duo on.

Briley held his arms wide, grinning arrogantly as the audience chanted his name. The pair were dressed in revealing bohemian style clothing, hearkening to medieval times. He had Dulce strapped to a wooden wall as he leered over her for some unspeakable crime she committed.

"This woman," He pointed at Dulce with his bow, puffing angrily, "Dared to practice sorcery in my kingdom." Briley bellowed.

The crowd ate it up and cheered back, "Treason! Kill her! She deserves to die!"

"Woman!" Briley stomped up to Dulce's face, barely a breath away from her, "Say your last words!"

I settled into the crowds around the duo. It was hard resisting the urge to heckle Briley.

Dulce's face twisted as she spit at him.

Briley proceeded in a rage, pacing back a few steps to draw an arrow and aim it at Dulce.

"Die you heathen!" He bellowed, letting the arrow loose.

It whizzed through the air, silencing the audience in suspense. As it fixed on its target, Dulce burst from her restraints and met the arrow head on. Where it should've buried itself through her forehead, it burst into a dozen monarch butterflies who fluttered to rest on the top of her head and shoulders.

It took another second for the crowd to process what had happened and remember how to breathe. Fascination then took over and rendered the lot to applause and enthused inquiries on how the feat was done.

Briley initially jutted his chin up and glowered down on his partner before a smirk formed on his lips. He held a hand out to Dulce that she accepted, and they bowed before throng of spectators.

I grinned and took the moment to retreat back to a food stand for a funnel cake while Briley and Dulce greeted their audience.

The wonder of how they'd done it would be left unanswered and unacknowledged. Not just to add to the mystique of the act, but because they did enjoy baffling people. Like the Ringmaster taunted in his opening speech every dream, there were people who couldn't help themselves but to find an explanation for everything. And the sideshow troupes in the carnival were scoundrels enough to purposefully master acts that people would drive themselves crazy in trying to figure out how it worked.

For all the time that I had worked here and despite my good friendship with a number of them, I had no idea how they did some of it either.

I appreciatively took my funnel cake heaped with an inhumane dose of powdered sugar and caramel.

When I turned back around to where the double side just finished, Dulce and Briley were slipping off into the venue tent. I followed suit.

"You want some funnel cake?" I offered, namely to Dulce.

She turned back and skipped over to me, "They always taste sweeter coming from you."

"Well it's my offering to the sorceress of the midway. Such a lovely performance as always." I reply as she strung an arm around my shoulders and walked with me towards the stage where Briley then cleared his throat pointedly. He was looking for his own wave of praise.

"I've said all I have to say." I grinned, plucking a piece of funnel cake and washing it down with stout. "By the way, I hate your brother."

"Why? He doesn't discriminate. He hates everyone equally." Briley reached forward and helped himself to my funnel cake, "Sorry, by the way, not for stealing your food, or for my brother, or for making you choke on beer. But you know… what happened to you."

His self-assertive voice faltered to a sort of bashful one, unsure of whether or not to broach the subject.

I chuckled, "Lement kissed and told?"

"No, I did." Dulce quipped, pecking me on the cheek before skipping off backstage, "I'm changing, then we're riding the carousel and getting frozen hot chocolate."

"Lame." Briley called after her before grinning back at me, "He had to." He said, referring to Lement, "When we went to get your stuff. You think that diva did it all by himself?"

"Well, thank you," I concurred, "But I still hate your brother."

The ruby colored contacts Briley wore, that somehow managed to be redder than his hair, glinted wickedly, "Who doesn't?"

SCENE SEVEN

"How dare you?!" Lement breathed, his face contorted into betrayal. "You're playing with them and not me?"

Briley and I were playing a water race carnival game where you shoot water at a target. Said target made an icon shoot to the top. Whoever got their icon to the top first, won the game.

I took the water shooting faux rifle and brought it to Lement's head. Consequently, Briley won the round for getting his icon to the top of the chute first. My eyes evenly met Lement's pale yellows, responding none whatsoever before pulling the trigger and dousing him with water.

The reaction that elicited was nothing more than a stern expression and his hands on his hips.

Dulce was sitting on the game counter, sipping on her frozen hot chocolate, "Because she likes me more than you."

Lement let out an agitated scoff as he rolled his eyes, "Because she likes me more than you." He mimicked childishly prior to pulling out his fart spray and encompassing her in a mist of it. The most delighted smile took his face as she squealed in disgust.

"Excuse me, I own her." Briley challenged the jester.

Lement smirked at Briley, "And I own you."

Briley beamed, "Can I call you daddy?"

At that, Lement cackled, "Why not? Your woman does."

"Who I do like more than you." I jested in Dulce's defense.

Lement spun on me, eyes bewildered, "But-"

"Oh, come on, doll face. It's just champagne." Dulce further taunted.

There had been a time where Lement got bent out of sorts again and thusly dumped a glass of champagne on Dulce. When she complained about it, his sole response was that it was 'just champagne' and therefore no big deal. Ever since, it became a running gag to quip "it's just champagne" whenever one of us wanted to challenge someone that it was no big deal.

"You're one to talk." Lement growled with a sarcastic smile. "Now, Nannette, friend—ooh, your hair!"

"If there's one perk to moving in here, it's that *you* won't strangle me for dying my hair," I retorted.

If he had heard my comment, he didn't respond to it. Instead, he twirled a mauve lock curiously. His eyes then flicked back up to mine.

"You look ridiculous, I love it."

I scoffed and crossed my arms, "I know damn well I look better than you could ever."

"She's not lying." Dulce added.

"Don't the two of you have a show in twenty?" Lement eyed both Dulce and Briley. Aforementioned Jack was silently downing the rest of Dulce's frozen hot chocolate before she could notice.

Briley's eyes bulged, but not in response to Lement. Unsurprisingly, he'd given himself a brain freeze.

"Mhm." The redhead offered as he reeled at the discomfort. Dulce merely gazed down at him with the corner of her mouth quirked.

"Serves you right." She ran a hand through her hair prior to winking at me as she departed to the dressing room, "You're still an eyesore, Lement."

I chuckled as Lement grimaced, "The people who *hate* me say otherwise."

Briley scrambled along after the Jackette, leaving Lement and I at the game stand. My eyes darted to the sling shot attraction at the screams of the couple on board. As much of a daredevil I was, I didn't trust the ride enough that a cable wouldn't snap. It made me shudder at the thought.

"It's happening." Lement remarked, noticing what I'd been staring at.

Immediately, my instincts to run like a bat out of hell took over. But Lement had already anticipated it. He scooped me up over his shoulder the very second I turned to bolt. I was left wriggling around in his grasp, protesting.

"No!" In my panic, I couldn't help but laugh anxiously, "Please, don't! I'll do whatever you say for a whole day or try to play your character for a set. I'll shave my head bald. Put me down!"

Lement found my despair and offers entertaining, "Oh, goodie! So, I put you down now and then you do whatever I say for a whole day. And I'll tell you to re-ride this thing from dusk to dawn."

I balked at that, "I should've listened to Myrtle. I didn't want to believe that you're as horrible as she says."

Lement didn't miss a beat, "She said that? I'm flattered."

"You aren't going to go harass her because I told you that?" I asked, humor dropping from my voice.

Lement snorted, "Now I can't promise I won't harass anyone because then I'd being lying and lying is wrong."

I struck his back with a fist, "Put me down!"

"No," He laughed, before continuing matter of fact, "Dollie doesn't like me. Never has, never will. A lot of people don't like me because I enjoy pissing them off. And, I will continue to piss them off to see at what point I can make a person break."

"Haven't I been through enough?"

At last, he paused. I could imagine his visible displeasure at me pulling that card. Not to waste the opportunity, I rolled to the left and managed to drop off of his shoulder. It wasn't the most graceful landing, but it was enough for me to tear off and away from my captor.

* * *

I successfully managed to evade Lement for the rest of the evening. It was not an easy feat despite the carnival's nooks and crannies. And it also meant missing out on the carnival chef's exceptional meal he'd serve to employees for dinner, but it spared me getting on the sling shot for at least another day. Which hopefully, was long enough for him to forget. A lot could happen in a day.

Lamely enough, for the last hour that the carnival was open, I tucked away in Annie's tent. I was afraid that I would get right up to the very end of the operating day and he'd catch me. Not that he paid his parents enough mind as he should, but I still felt safest there. Annie would probably be able to foresee him coming or something cliché.

Nonetheless, I was safely walking down the midway to the airstream park.

Despite it having just closed, it was a ghost town. That wasn't in reference to the guests that usually filled the carnival but rather the employees who made it run.

I had closed it a few times before, but typically got off an hour or two before closing for the sake of my adoptive parents' sanity. Them not knowing that Lement and his family ran this carnival was another detail I liked to chalk up as being for their sanity's sake too. As was me only using my airstream on nights when they were out of town on a business trip or I'd told them I was staying with Myrtle.

In the handful of times that I had closed, it never really struck me how fast closing out was. Since this carnival didn't open until early afternoon, they opted to do the bulk of the afterhours work then when there was daylight. It was a win-win situation. Employees can tap out earlier than they would otherwise, and I can enjoy the midway to myself in peace.

The overhead music was already off, giving way for the last few game stands' music to harmonize together. The lights at the rides were still on. The Ferris wheel glowed deep red against the night sky and the zipper loomed menacingly with its golden lights framing it.

I was not remotely ashamed to say that I would ride the zipper, and have done so in fact, but will not ride the sling shot. Period. Maybe that was ridiculous considering the zipper was an unforgiving ride for the masochistic with a deafening roar to add to its intimidating stature. But despite that, I stood my ground firmly.

The rides' engines were still humming in anticipation of the next ride cycle. The mechanics must not come through to shut them down for a little bit after closing. It might've been easier on the rides' systems, but the mechanical side to rides was not my area of expertise.

A long hiss from the octopus ride momentarily startled me as I gazed at the zipper. Compressed air had found its way out of the machinery. The lights on the arms did a dance and alternated colors in a little show of its own.

The ensuing thud and squeaking behind me made me jump out right. It was a curse to be someone who scared easily.

It was just a car from the Funhouse, an old school dark ride, reemerging to the loading platform through a door.

I chuckled at myself. These were all noises that the rides emitted during the day, but I likely hadn't paid any mind to them with the noise of the music and crowds largely drowning them out. I swallowed down the lingering and ridiculous sense of unease.

Even if it was for the shortest period of time, I was living at a carnival. As such, perks innately included getting to explore the rides at night. And, although I'd ridden the Funhouse before, it was one of the few attractions that I hadn't worked yet. Now was as good as time as any to explore it.

I slipped under the railings of the queue and stepped up to the loading platform. The yellow and white striped cars patiently waited in a single file line for their next passengers.

I didn't know the first thing about running this particular attraction so poking around by foot would have to do. And ideally, staying on the outskirts of the ride path lest another cart fancied itself on another round of its own accord.

The loading platform wasn't but seven yards long, give or take. Just long enough for half a dozen carts to sit outside on the platform while the others waited just inside the show building, on the other side of the wooden exit door. For its portable nature, the majority of the Funhouse was still made of wood. It didn't seem like it'd be as easy to transport, but somehow the Radus managed it.

I pressed through the entry door into the show building. Upon stepping into the first scene room, I was met with an endless number of my reflections.

Right off the bat, it went with the stereotypical hall of mirrors schtick. What little bits of the walls that could be seen were black. The mirrors stretched from the ceiling to the floor, each one lined by vibrantly colored trim. Ultraviolet lighting made them glow in the dark. And, pretty much impossible to see where the ride's guide track ran to find the way to the next room. Looks like I was going to have to hug the track.

Carefully, I extended a foot towards where the track would be. The last thing I wanted to do was go and damage a part of the ride. It was easy and quick enough to feel out. Like a tight rope walker, except with my foot along the side of the rail instead of on top of it, I let the track guide me forward.

There were several turns in this scene alone. As apparently, it wasn't just one big space leading to the next door. It was a series of disorienting twists and near misses, so a rider truly had no idea which way was the right way. It was devious. I liked that.

Along the side of my feet that were brushing against the track's rail, it felt as if it was ever so slightly vibrating. Like the outdoor rides hummed and blew compressed air, the dark ride was trembling before bed. What point was it that the mechanics came around to turn them off?

It was easy to tell when I approached the next room as there was a break in the mirrors. It was another door. That was a charm the older attractions had. They lacked the creative way of concealing one section from another. The older ones were simple. They just put up a door for the cars to run into and push open by themselves.

Upon seeing the theme of the second scene, I laughed. It was a vivid haven of clowns, a sensory overload of every neon, glow in the dark hue in the rainbow. All sorts of shapes, gag props, mannequins, and lighting gave the colorful room a substantial amount of kinetic energy. It was the type to draw out the wildness in anyone.

Mania. That was a good word for it.

This room was worth exploring. It also featured its fair share of nooks and crannies. It was a wonder Briley didn't live here. His airstream was the source of inspiration for this scene.

"Hehehe!"

"Shit." I breathed, dropping against an orange wall with a hand to my chest.

One of the mannequins evidently had a sensor attached to it to emit a doll-like sinister giggle when activated. That would've been great to know. Maybe the older attractions still received their respective bit of newer luxuries.

I started to laugh at myself. Again, it was a curse to scare so easily.

Straightening myself out, I wandered up to the mannequin the giggle had come from. He was a bright, cheerful looking clown. Fortunately, a world's different from the ones at Cirque Arcana. Everything within the carnival was nothing short of a burst of jovial extraordinary. The king of carnivals, belittling every cliché you'd imagine like it wasn't spectacular enough.

It went pitch black.

My breath hitched in my throat as it fully registered. Considering my wondering about when the mechanics shut the rides down, I should've expected that at any moment. But that would require me thinking things through and that was not something I was known for.

I bit my bottom lip. I could feel my way along the track to the front since I was only in the second scene, but I was not liking the darkness and the silence. With each passing second, I was that much closer to completely freaking out. It simply didn't settle well with me. For whatever reason that was, being alone in the Funhouse with no power was the most uncomfortable thing to me since Nick.

"Hehehe!"

It's sad to say, but I dropped to the ground again.

"No!" I told the inanimate being. I didn't know where the sensor was, but I didn't want to unintentionally trigger the thing again.

I took a deep breath, "Grow a pair." I huffed to myself before standing up once more. It was back to feeling along the track with my feet.

It was at that second that the edge of my foot found the rail, that the squeak of one of the wooden doors broke the silence. The ride was off. That was not a car. And it wasn't me.

"Bullshit," I stumbled against the wall behind me and blindly grabbed the first piece of set décor that I touched. It was a bowling pin.

I had not the slightest notion as to what I was defending myself from, but it was my first instinct. Fight or flight? I chose both.

The bowling pin took on a newfound roll of a hybrid between a sword and a baseball bat. I held it out, ready to swing at the next source of sound.

I inched forward slowly, "What is that?" I whispered to myself, then blindly shouted, "Who's there?"

It was instinct rather than rationality that fueled me at the moment. If it were the ride or a rogue racoon, they wouldn't respond. But on the off chance that there was another person, they'd reply.

I took another cautious step forward.

The wooden door behind me that led to the third scene squeaked now as it was opened. Reflexively, I beamed the bowling pin at it. A sad thud and the sound of the pin falling to the ground ensued.

I couldn't tell whether the next sound was shushing or compressed air. But the sound after that I knew for certain was me screaming as I scrambled back, crouching on the ground.

"What the hell are you doing in here?"

Out of nowhere, Lement was shining a flashlight down on me. The amusement was evident in his voice. I was glad that I couldn't see it in his face.

"Getting ready to crack your head with a bowling pin," I launch myself into him, sending him back a pace.

Filled with mirth, he proceeded to tickle my waste to get me off of him. He was successful.

"You're an ass, Lement!"

"You are what you eat."

I ran a hand through my hair, "This is payback? I didn't get on the ride with you."

Lement snorted in glee, "Yet is the keyword, Nannette. Now did you go tearing up the set?"

It was too dark for him to see the innocent, apologetic smile on my face, "Eh?"

"Eh?" He laughed dryly, "'Eh?' She says."

I could hear him shift around as he panned his flashlight, presumably trying his best to assess what I'd disturbed.

"It's just the bowling pin," I offered, now hoping that I hadn't messed anything up. It was easy not to care in the heat of the moment of freaking out. But outside of that window, I knew it'd be disrespectful to mess up an attraction after his family took me in, "I threw it at the door you pushed."

"Which one?" He asked.

"Scene three."

Somewhere in the dark oblivion, I could hear Lement acquire the prop in question and return it to its proper place.

"Lovely," He mused, turning back to me, "I wasn't at that door, because *I* wasn't snooping around the dark ride."

I scoffed, "Right."

As Lement had returned to me, I could see his eyebrow lift, "You're crazy, Nannette."

"You were pushing around on the doors," My face balled up at the jester, "You probably cut the lights off too because you knew I was in here."

Lement smirked, "It's the end of the night, Estela. The rides shut down. You probably heard the other door that I came through from scene one. You want to go outside now?"

I didn't believe Lement for a second. It was *Lement*, Lement.

"Yeah, sure." I repeated skeptically.

SCENE EIGHT

Dulce rolled her eyes and smiled, knowingly. I had just recalled the previous night's pit stop at the Funhouse with her as we relaxed atop the Jacks & Jackettes' green room. The sun was still working its way up the sky. I hadn't slept properly the night before and my other best friend was an early bird.

The bad sleep was worth it though. I wasn't sure how often I'd be up so early here, but the sunrise over the carnival was beautiful. It was a visual token of the better days ahead. Days that didn't include Melissa and Nick. Days that didn't mean I had to walk on egg shells at home. Days that meant that I could just be me.

She rolled over and rested her cheek in her hand, "It's about time." She mused to herself, looking up at me strangely.

I grinned, confused and curious. I could already tell it was something she was deciding upon herself. She always got that look when she was about to tell a tale Lement wouldn't be enthused about. Those were my favorite tales.

"It is time." Came my reply, "For what?"

The roguish glimmer in her chocolate eyes furthered my excitement.

Dulce bit her bottom lip, "Lement wasn't screwing around with you in the Funhouse."

"Okay?" The excited anticipation outweighed the voice in my head from last night that wondered if it wasn't Lement, then who was it?

"And you don't want to poke around the attractions after close." She then sobered, "Seriously, do not do that."

"Okay?" The anticipation subsided only ever so slightly.

In the next second, the raven-haired woman whipped out a throwing knife and held it out to me, "Press it against your finger, baby doll."

While most people would have questioned that, I obeyed without hesitation. A fine line leaked blood from the top tip of my finger to where it creased. I held out my finger to show Dulce before popping it in my mouth to suck the blood off of it.

"Right?" Dulce noted before taking the knife back and holding it at her wrist, prepared to cut her arm open vertically.

"Wait, what-"

She pressed the knife firmly into her skin and drug it down to her elbow before I could appropriately protest her intentions. Her skin showed the clear signs that the knife had pushed into it, but it didn't split open.

It was now me biting my lips, "The hell?"

Dulce beamed before then pulling a match, lighting it, and holding her hand directly in the flame. As my face frowned further into bewilderment, she proceeded to drop the match into her mouth and breathe fire. She then took the match and bit it between her teeth for me to see.

If someone had asked me how I would've reacted to that before seeing it, I'd have said that I'd love it. I'd want to learn how. It'd be the coolest thing ever. Finally, something exciting. Something that defied what was supposed to be possible. That was my life's ambition.

But having just seen it, I felt the complete opposite. My eyes literally just watched her try to cut herself open, try to burn herself, and eat fire just to breathe it like a dragon without any kerosene or whatever it was that they used during shows.

And yet, my mind was not accepting it. Who's to say what was and wasn't possible, but my psyche was adamantly against what she'd just done. Even despite having just seen it. There was an incomplete connection between what my eyes saw and what my brain processed.

That left my body unsure of how to feel about it. Part of me wanted to laugh and be in awe while the other part was thoroughly disturbed and unamused. As such, my face settled into a frown.

"You've been here so long, you live here now, you're practically family, and you're about to turn eighteen so you might as well know about it so you can decide for yourself." She began with a small smile, "Do you want to live forever?"

I still sat silently dumbfounded, causing her to laugh.

"There's no way of doing this without it being cheesy as hell. You're going to think I'm kidding and I'm really not."

An anxious chuckle escaped me, "Get on with it."

Dulce smirked, "Where to begin?" She mulled over before grinning at me again. She knew how direct I was, most of the time, to a fault. I wasn't one for beating around the bush and eloquence.

"Let's start with last night," She began, "All of the attractions have a sentience about them. It just kind of developed over time considering this is a hub of magic. It took on its own sort of life. But the magic accentuates good and bad to extremes. More often than not it leans towards bad since it lacks empathy, compassion, a moral compass itself.

Magic is alive in the sense plants and nature are. It's not conscientiously thinking, it's just being. Now certain things can take on a consciousness after being… I don't know. Like the Funhouse, it's sat in a hub of magic since the 1940s. It being in the middle of it, the magic just kind of built up into it, so to speak. How's that for a start?"

I sat silently for another moment before laughing incredulously. I didn't disbelieve her; I just had no idea of what to make of any of it.

"…then the Funhouse can eat me alive." I laughed, overwhelmed by how crazy it seemed, before sliding off the top of the green room. Here it was barely eight in the morning and now I wanted a drink. But instead of heading for a stout, I made my way to Lement's trailer to ask the one I knew to be the expert of all things crazy.

I took out my bobby pin that I kept on hand, technically in hair, for reasons such as this and picked the lock on his door. Unceremoniously, I welcomed myself into his airstream.

"Lemmy!" I called knowing he hated the nick name, but not as much as he hated his full name. Seeing as the living area was empty, I barged into his bedroom.

"Lemmy!" I repeated.

"Piss off." He whined from underneath his pillow and covers. I sat on top of his back.

"And get your fat ass off me." He added.

I smirked, "Good morning, Mr. Radu. I'm here to inquire why you've lied to my face?"

My voice remained level, so no emotion could bleed through. I wasn't sure what to do with my emotions at the moment anyhow.

"Get. Your. Fat. Ass. Off. Me." He repeatedly, muffled in the cushions.

I glared down at where his head was hidden underneath the pillow. Out of the corner of my eye, Dulce peering in the airstream doorway briefly stole my attention.

"If I get up, it's to leave and not come back."

Lement remained quiet. He'd either dozed off or was wondering if I was being serious or not. Dulce stepped just inside the airstream but remained further back. I flashed her a smile.

"I'm in the onset of an existential crisis right now. I'm glad you don't care." I added for good measure.

Lement shifted, he was awake. He spun around on his back, propelling me off of him. I stumbled to prevent myself from falling into the floor. He gave me a peculiar look before it soured and flitted to Dulce.

"And what do *you* want?" It was another rare instant where he was talking normally.

Dulce shrugged innocently, "I'm just here making sure my friend who's going through an existential crisis is okay."

Lement snorted incredulously and looked back to me, "What lie?"

"You tell me."

His eyes flicked over to Dulce and back to me once more, he was unimpressed, "Okay," He sat up, leaning against the backboard, "I've never liked you. I find you repulsive, disgusting. I don't know why I put up with you, really. You're the bane of my existence, terror in my nightmares..."

With a sigh, I ran a hand through my freshly dyed hair and sat on his floor cross legged, "Everything I thought was bull is real. Everything I thought was real is bull. You know, I truly wouldn't be surprised if you do hate me."

Lement's face fell into concern, "What's going on, Nannette?"

I couldn't help the dry laugh that escaped me, "That's what I'm asking you, Lement."

His jaw clenched and he swung to sit on the edge of the bed facing me, his mouth was in a firm line, "When am I serious?"

I half shrugged.

"I don't hate you." His eyebrows raised, hazel eyes sincere, "Why would I hate you?"

Dulce took a step closer to the two of us.

"I once thought that my parents loved me. I once thought magic was a pipe dream." I chuckled, a discomfort residing in my chest, "But I've had two sets of parents tell me I'm not worth loving. And then, my best friend goes and lights herself on fire, but doesn't because something, something the Funhouse is sentient."

Lement's face lit up with the most pleasant, sardonic smile to grace the planet. His head slowly tilted to Dulce.

"De Leche…" He spoke through his teeth, still glowing. He batted his eyelashes for good measure, "I love you."

Two fingers then pinched the bridge of his nose, "Please… go outside…"

"It's an inevitability." Dulce noted, unapologetic.

Lement chuckled darkly, "Maybe, but not for the best. It's kind of messy given that she's what? Only three days in from leaving her toxic parents?"

Dulce gave a slight nod, concurring, as I remained on the floor impatiently.

"Sure, pumpkin, but whether we like this timing or not, she's far in." She grimaced before grinning, "Besides, you're being overdramatic. What's the harm in telling her that your yellow eyes aren't contacts?"

At that, I broke out in the most incredulous, exasperated laugh, "So help me… what?!" I couldn't stop giggling in disbelief at this point, "Are you guys even being real right now?"

Dulce took a seat on Lement's bed next to him. The latter of whom was now smirking. His thought process always took the back seat when it came to the opportunity of screwing with someone. That was too much fun for rationality to hamper it.

"Okay, you want it real quick?" Lement's jester voice was back. "Mull it over? Come back for details and questions?"

Dulce elbowed him with a grin, prompting him to go on. That only unintentionally delayed Lement a minute longer.

"Ow?" He questioned childishly before launching her off the end of his bed. Dulce glared at him playfully as she reclaimed her seat.

"Why do you have to sit so close to me? I'm not Briley."

"Screw me, man." I groaned to Lement's amusement.

"Not for free." He quipped, enjoying the sour look he was met with.

"Magic's real," He finally stated, "I'm literally a jester, she's literally a Jackette. I was born in 1932, she was born in 1948. I can teleport, she can light herself on fire. The Funhouse is sentient. It was likely going to trap you inside and keep you as it's plaything for the night. The Founders that your parents know? They're of magic too. Cirque Arcana? Same deal."

There it was. It sounded so absurd, but Dulce had just lit herself on fire without harm. My mind wanted to analyze it or block it out. I still didn't know how to feel about it.

The prospect of magic being real was a great thought. How much fun it would be… how much more exciting it was than the regular world. Once the initial mental cluster subsided and came to terms with it, there was no doubt that I'd be so ecstatic that I wouldn't know what to do with myself.

But it still didn't feel real. Nothing felt real. It still felt like a joke.

The question was, how much time was I going to waste trying to figure it out and come to terms with it? Whatever the truth was, it was. There was no changing it, so it'd be better to adapt now with it and move forward.

"Then teleport." I commanded Lement, it would be the fastest way for my mind to move towards accepting it and trusting that they weren't pranking me.

A mischievous smirk took his face before he vanished. There were no flashy or mystical effects to it. He didn't disappear in a cloud of smoke or in a blip of light. He was just there and now he wasn't.

I couldn't help but scoff, "Got it."

My icy colored eyes drifted from where Lement was to where Dulce currently sat, a grin adorning her face as well.

"So where do you think he went?" I asked, still in shock.

Before she could respond, a party horn unfurled next to my right ear with the most excited fanfare to come from an inanimate object. Me being me, I scrambled into a ball on the floor. And in classic Lement fashion, a cloud of glitter rained down on my pathetic state.

"Congratulations! Now you know. So, think it over? And the meantime, get out of my airstream." He beamed, "I love you, Nannette!"

I begrudgingly sat up and gave him the same playful glare he'd just received from Dulce.

"Oh, thank you, kind sir." I feigned sarcasm to hide my state of shock.

Lement stood straight and bowed before jutting his chin up, "I'll find you in a bit once I'm finished fully waking up and skinning Dulce alive for stirring this all up at such an unforgiving hour."

He offered a hand to which I accepted, and he pulled me up to my feet. I already had a surplus of questions. He'd only given a short summary, but that short summary was like a nuclear bomb.

So, my reoccurring dream… Cirque Arcana was real? Like… *Cirque Arcana* was real? Why did Cirque Arcana want anything to do with me? The Founders worked with my parents, was that coincidence? Dulce and Lement were how old? What the hell?

…

What the hell?

The questions that already sprung to mind were never ending. But there was one that I immediately wanted to know. My sweet best friend had a strange disdain for my eccentric one.

"And Myrtle?"

Dulce looked up curiously at Lement, likewise intrigued at his answer. I supposed Dulce knew Myrtle too. How many of my friends from, theoretically, different circles knew each other?

"Oh," Lement chuckled, "She knows. That's why she hates me."

"How?"

"That's a Myrtle question." The wry smirk was back. He enjoyed my loss.

A small smile formed on my lips, "Well, good sir, I'll bombard you in a bit."

Lement's face balled up in faux disgust, "Ew."

Dulce rolled her eyes, "I'll see you, baby doll."

Giving a nod, I headed out of Lement's airstream, leaving a trail of glitter raining down from me.

The air outside seemed different now. A lingering anxiety still resided in my chest. Seeing the carnival, onstage and backstage, looked different now. I was trying to discern how I felt about that.

Things before weren't necessarily a lie. I didn't feel any differently about Dulce or Lement. Their lives were their lives. They likely couldn't go around dropping the bomb shell of magic to just anyone. I didn't feel any sort of deception from them. But from the carnival itself, I did.

It hadn't blatantly lied to me before if it was capable of doing so. But it was now missing two things I cherished most about it that I couldn't get at home.

Safety.

Trust.

* * *

"It's parade day!" Lement chirped excitedly.

Said jester wore black, white, and yellow striped clothes. The top looked like a long-sleeved button up nightshirt while his bottoms were matching pants. If his shirt had been tucked in, it would've looked like he was wearing a one piece due to the precise alignment of the stripes. It was an odd look that complimented Lement's personality.

"Nice pajamas." I remarked.

Lement scoffed in mock offense, "It is not pajamas, it is a suit."

I mimicked his voice, "It's not pajamas, it's a suit."

Lement's hand shot forward to my side to tickle me before he effortlessly tossed me over his shoulder and turned to head deeper into the maze of airstreams. I was left to limply ride on his shoulder to his intended destination.

"Are you really 80-something years old?" I figured it was as good a time as ever to continue where we'd left off.

After all, it was supposed to continue once he was squared away for the day. He apparently had other plans now.

"Yes? No? I don't know." He replied, still skipping along, "I stopped aging at 23. Mentally, physically, and whatnot. But I've been on this earth for sixty years longer. I don't have that infinite wisdom or whatever the hell eighty-year-olds have. But, I also don't have a walker. Because technically, I'm still 23."

"Can you die?" My intention was innocent, a curiousness on how the living but not aging thing worked. But when the spring in his step faltered, I realized how it probably came across.

"Damn." He huffed sourly.

"I mean like, are you going to basically live forever unless something happens to you?" While my voice was light, the apologetic tone was evident.

Lement cackled, "Aw, are you counting me out just yet?"

"I don't want to. I very much prefer you alive."

Lement set me down. We were at the Rounds.

"Most people don't." He smiled wickedly, "But I'd have to untether from the magic or be killed by someone who could actually do it to die. And trust me, people have tried. But I'm kinda hard to kill."

I didn't like the thought and I was certain my face showed it.

"What's tether?" I inquired, preferring to focus on that end.

"It's how you become of magic; you tether to it, like bonding yourself to it." He explained before adding dramatically, "It owns your soul."

I batted my lashes at Lement, "I own your soul."

"Oh, you can try." His ever-present wicked smirk reappeared, "And, good luck with that."

He then took a fist and pounded the green room door of the Jacks & Jackettes.

"Kellan!" He bellowed before taking it upon himself to kick in the door without giving anyone the chance to open it.

My face soured as I groaned, "Why Kellan?"

Lement's light yellow eyes glanced back to me wildly, "Because Kellan's ingenious. Aren't you Kellan?"

The ill mood redhead was sitting at the antique lounge table. In one hand, held the phone he was browsing through looking at God knows what, more than likely what the cruelest way of killing someone was. In the other hand, a carving knife slid over the next upside-down shot glass before being stabbed into it, effectively shattering the shards about the table and the floor. Then rinse and repeat.

One red eyebrow peaked, and ruby eyes lazily wandered to us and then back to the phone.

His eyes were naturally red.

* * *

Oh.

A giggling fit then took hold of me. To Lement's curiosity and Kellan's ambivalence.

"That's so fitting!" I muster between laughs, "His eyes." Lement looked towards Kellan who remained disinterested. That just poked, ever so slightly, the right button to make me throw cynicism back at him and recall the previous day's conversation, "Can your dead mother walk yet after my nonexistent father was done with her?"

Kellan begrudgingly gave us his attention once more to meet my stare and Lement's utter fascination.

"Dear, friends," The jester- oh, the literal jester evidently, lit up, "It's time to join the festivities. In other words, Kellan stop being a pissant and Nannette, be nice."

"Aren't I nice?" I grin at him.

He matched it, "If you're nice, I'm sane, and Kellan's a saint."

I chuckled, "I'm nice! Just not to Kellan. I was actually trying to be nice to you when I last talked to him to make sure I had the appropriate mindset going forward." I explained, donning a made up, sophisticated accent, "I had a few questions, just to make sure I'd be sensitive and respectful. He was the one to-"

"Tell her to piss off to the daddy that dumped her, not to be confused with the one who beats her." Kellan finished, a resilient frown on his face.

Lement turned on him, highly unamused. He started to say something but stopped to tilt his head back to me, "Step outside for a second, Nannette?"

The corner of my lips creeped up as I looked from Lement to Kellan, "Sure."

I made an effort to watch my step on the downed green room door and stepped out.

This was a rare Lement. Undoubtedly, he was pissed. But the only way you could tell was the peeved twitch in his eye. His voice remained in the quirky jester accent- or maybe that was his natural voice?

It was a surreal new era of time where the only reason why I seemed fine with the bomb that was dropped on me this morning was because I hadn't suitably processed it yet. It didn't feel real still.

Somewhere inside me knew that it was. But the large part of me took it as an inside joke or odd game.

Anyhow, Lement never got angry. He'd likely just tell someone off in a chipper voice, restrained from shouting and profanities. Profanities were for joking and casual talk, so he said.

But it wasn't any less satisfying to see Kellan in the doghouse. It was where he belonged. Call me whatever, I could be frank and callous sometimes between the general eclectic extrovert. But Kellan was straight up heartless to everyone. I had no idea why Lement was best buddies with him. Maybe there was a point in time when Kellan wasn't so unpleasant.

The hair on the back of my neck decided to stand on end. I already knew it was me psyching myself out before I looked around the Rounds. I'd come to find out about certain things being sentient and now my subconcious felt like everything and anything was watching me.

Sure enough, the Rounds was clear save for the clowns' green room ruins. I sighed to myself and ran a hand through my mauve hair.

What was life anymore?

A reassuring thought was Kellan stayed in a perpetual state of misery. That would never change.

Lement appearing in the green room doorway caught the corner of my eye. As he said a final word to the Jack, it dawned on me that I hadn't heard so much as Lement's voice although the door was gone.

So, how the hell was I three years into being here and never had any sort of clue or strange occurrence to tip me off until now?

Just in three days, magic became the new normal.

Time to accept it and move on, Sinclair. I wasn't the type to care for dwelling on things.

"Moving along," Lement pranced out of the green room and offered an arm. "Care to join the sensible people?"

"What are sensible people?" I took his arm.

SCENE NINE

The rest of the morning to a little after midday was spent busy with the undertaking of the monster that was parade prep.

Of course, it wasn't only a single day preparation sort of event. It consisted of a few months of designing, creating, training, rehearsing, and executing.

The creative teams got to work on the overarching theme and style of the parade itself. That then branched into how each float would look. Whether or not the floats would incorporate custom features such as aerial rigs, trap doors, pyro effects, and so forth.

And then a similar deal with the costumes. What themes for which acts? Subsequently designing costumes for each troupe of performers, as well as tailoring costumes to the particular acts. Most were complex, as lively as the Midway itself.

The operators of the floats naturally were trained on them. But, the performers had to be trained on their costumes as well. Some required being on a hoverboard sort of thing that was hidden under the skirt of the outfit. Others were hooked into harnesses that essentially turned the performer into an attraction itself.

For example, this parade's theme was 'Off the Midway.' As all of the parades are, it's a two-hour route from the Midway into town and back in time for the carnival to open.

With this theme, a number of the float leads, the performers spearheading a float, were the various attractions.

The carousel float lead had a miniature replica attached to them. The replica was a functioning, spinning little carousel, with brightly colored jumping horses, that had a vertical tunnel through the center so the performer could wear it. Said performer had to be hoisted up over and then down into the replica where it'd be hooked onto the performer's waist harness. It spanned from the waist to just above the knees. So, once the performer was in it, they were in it. There was no sitting down or taking big strides.

Another float lead portrayed the swings. This performer was dressed in a body suit decorated to resemble the ride's center column. They were then put in an embellished harness that had a pole jutting up a few feet to hold the crossbeams from which the small replica swings hung. Again, it was the full nine yards, a model with an entirely operational ride system. As in, yes, the thing actually swung. It had a motorized panel in the harness to pull it all off. To boot, the crossbeams were connected to the pole with a swivel so the performer could also twirl independently of the replica.

It was pretty awing to see the costume and mechanical teams work together to create the great many of them. Other leads included one with the zipper attraction replica hooked to their back, one with a ferris wheel hovering above their head with its two feet mounted on either shoulder, and another with an octopus model attached to their waist. And, of course, all were fully functional.

"Here we are, Nannette!"

Lement whipped a curtain back to reveal the rainbow overload I was to wear.

"You're going to pretend to be one of the clowns who thinks she's going to take over my place, but she's oh so wrong." He explained teasingly, "I'll throw your ass off the float."

"Be my guest," I grinned, "That'll be a nice lawsuit for my birthday. You'll set me up well."

The jester laughed, "Great game plan. Get changed so Bex can take you up before we start."

Bex Paramo was the director of entertainment at the carnival. Fortunately, she was far more pleasant to deal with than John, the operations manager who routinely chastised employees and children. The blonde was also so passionate about theater and her performers that she was often seen on the frontlines, or technically the closest thing to front lines when you're still backstage. On top of overseeing the department in its entirety, she also helped stagehands and stage managers at the top of a show. At times, she stepped in as a swing when necessary.

"Gotcha." I replied as I whisked inside the dressing space.

We were in the general dressing room. It was a massive counterpart to the individual dressing rooms, by the sideshows, explicitly for such events as these. There were several dressing spaces tucked aside in the dressing room. It was mandatory for minors for the good reasons one would expect.

Inside my dressing space my colorful costume hung alongside a makeup chart depicting my face paint. My makeup was, needless to say, in tune with the rest of my costume. I would have the clown white foundation with pink and purples contouring my cheeks, blue contouring my nose, pink and purple overdrawn lips, blue eyebrows, and rainbow eyeshadow that stretched from my blue brows to my pink cheeks. They went overboard with the design, so I was going to be unrecognizable even to myself.

The costume was pulled last minute from the costumes shop. For a split-second addition, no one would tell. All of the costumes were intricate spectacles of themselves. As such, there was no way anyone would grab a random assortment out of the shop and it not look as if it were seamlessly part of the show or event from the start. It made it perfect for no-notice drop ins such as me.

This wasn't anywhere near the first parade for me. My work at the carnival was always split between ride operations and special events. But due to the unforeseen circumstances that brought me here sooner than usual, I was cast into the parade. Hence the convenience of having friends in high places. High carnival places, that was.

My alternative was to stay behind at the carnival. And while fun, it wasn't as fun as the monthly parade *and* the carnival. Not to mention, I had no idea just all of what was borderline sentient, or whatever. I didn't need my airstream to start pulling the antics the Funhouse did.

And while I could spectate the parade from the crowds, I had to be incognito in public. No one outside of the carnival crew would recognize my face when it was done up like the clown queen of rainbows. So, should Melissa or Nick correctly assume I'd be somewhere in the midst of said parade, they wouldn't know which clown, knife thrower, or magician was me. The best sort of hiding was hiding in plain sight.

I quickly changed from the closest thing I had to regular clothes into the costume. It started with the stark white tights that had various primary colors of paint splattered about them. Then came the fluffy, tattered multi-layer polychrome tulle skirt. Up top was a white puffy blouse that had also been speckled in a healthy dose of colors. Rainbow suspenders layered over top from the skirt's waste band. A polka dot bow at my neck, teal bowler hat, and chunky purple heels completed the look.

Ready for makeup and Bex, I exited the dressing space.

* * *

This parade was one of my favorites yet. And, that wasn't entirely on account of the costume being the least complicated one I'd worn to date. I got to have a field day 'overthrowing' the carnival's jester. Naturally, I went all out with that.

Bex gave me a big, bright yellow fanny pack filled with rainbow glitter. One use was for simply twirling around and sprinkling it everywhere within reach. Secondly, on either side of the jester's throne were air jets along the floor. It was initially intended to add dramatic flair to Lement's costume and make it whip wildly about. For me though, I threw the tinsel into them so there was a lingering cloud of sparkles enshrouding me. Thirdly, anytime Lement came over to drag me from his throne, I gave him a dose of his own medicine.

Unbeknownst to him, the glitter wasn't all that I was armed with. I had asked Bex a favor that she was more than happy about.

I hadn't utilized it just yet though. I wanted him to get comfortable in a routine before catching him off guard. Unpredictability was another art form I had learned from my dear friend.

Aforementioned friend was busy weaving in and out of the scaled down scenes from the Madhouse. At the very front right of the float was a spiral slide he'd fly through down into a ball pit that hovered off the edge of the float. He'd jump out of that back onto the float where a spinning disk welcomed him. After a few tricks on that, he'd leap up into the revolving barrel of fun that sat on a platform in the middle center of the float. That led to the span of tilting floor panels and twisting stairs that ran from the front left of the float up to the back of the float where his favorite scene resided.

The back third of the float consisted of the obstacle course. It was a hybrid of wooden and inflatable elements that any parent wished they had to tire their children out before bed. Everyone else was simply exhausted by looking at it.

It was a labyrinth of beams, trap doors, holes, walls, nets, a bish bash, and bungee cords separated by ultraviolet lit corridors. Lement spent most of his time twisting about the course, poking out occasionally to antagonize me.

The throne I'd taken over was up on a podium that overlooked the rest of the float. The throne chair was hooked to a motor on the floor that tilted it on its back hinges at a near 45-degree angle periodically. I'd worked out the timing so that I'd jump on the chair, one foot planted on the back of the chair and the other on its seat while I celebrated my new, soon to be short lived, reign.

I was in the middle of that very moment when Lement sprung out of the obstacle course at me.

"You traitor to the crown!" He accused; his face filled with overexaggerated outrage. The yellow and black spiked diamonds over his eyes, reddish purple shading under them, and overdrawn black smile managed to make him look wilder than he already did.

"You're old hat!" I shot back, my own voice higher pitched.

His distaste intensified, "Water break." He growled quietly through his teeth.

My chin extended up, "I'm fine. I'm the clown queen! Now, shoo!"

Lement grinned and hauled me off of his throne, "Off with your head!"

I wriggled and kicked in Lement's grip to no avail. I was fine regarding needing water, but he wasn't accepting it.

He carried me into a small corridor at the base of the throne's platform. It led into the first floor of the obstacle course and was just out of sight for the audience.

"Drink." Lement commanded as he sat me down next to a water bottle with my name. I hadn't even brought one aboard the float. I was used to working the ground where we didn't have anywhere to put bottles, so we loaded up on hydrating beforehand.

I took a swig of water, "How's your arthritis doing, old man?"

"Better than you'll be doing when you're my age." He smirked, sitting opposite of me. "I do this all day, every day."

"Way to count me out, Lemuel." I replied, causing him to quirk an eyebrow in interest.

"What? Are you going to join?" He inquired between sips of his own water.

I shrugged, "I might. It depends on the finer details of it."

Lement chuckled, "It's not all bad," He had an amused grin, "Really, you'd love it. I know it has its… moments? How to-"

"It's screwed up," I interjected, cutting to the chase, "Dulce said magic has no moral code. Cirque

Arcana, that you've apparently known was real all this time, is a fantastic example of that. Did you know they paint their faces with blood there?"

Lement nodded in agreement, "Hence why I didn't want to burden you with something I can protect you from. You don't need to worry about any of that."

I grimaced, "Spare yourself. You've got indefinite time. I'll probably drop off the face of the earth sooner than later."

My dark humor at that spontaneously dissipated as I remembered Mildred, "Sorry, that's stupid."

"Well, you are stupid," Lement countered, flicking one of the bells on the tip of his hat, "And you don't get a choice in the matter. You're not allowed to die."

"Oh?" I questioned.

"Oh." He confirmed before continuing, "Magic's not something you can underestimate, but you won't have to worry about that." He gave a small smile, "But you are going to have to worry about me throwing your ass off my float still."

I snorted, "That again? You know what, good sir?"

"What?" Came his ever so smug reply.

I pulled a miniature can of spray paint that Bex kindly provided and doused him in red paint.

***

With a freshly made mug of steamed vanilla milk, I took a seat at the booth, in my airstream, that doubled as the dining table.

After the parade had finished, I opted to return 'home' to shower and change into a fresh set of clothes. Then the idea of steamed vanilla milk sounded great. It was something I had when I was little to settle before going to bed. It was soothing, calming. And, I needed peace at the moment.

While I didn't like dwelling, I still wasn't fully settled with the sizeable information that got dropped on me in the morning. I wanted to carry on as if everything was as it had been. And, a part of me was, but I had to sort through the bombshell that I was magic sounded absurd in my head. But here we are.

The existence of magic was jarring only in the sense of how unexpected and surreal the revelation was. Beyond the surprise, I didn't have any sort of feelings or thoughts to that end. Magic was magic.

Evidently it's not as lighthearted and whimsical as fairytales are inclined, but it was still something wonderous and frankly, exciting. It would be cool to explore it more.

The next point was tethering. By some sort of endeavor, you could quintessentially bind your soul to the magic and then be 'of' magic. Presumably, this was what Lement had meant when he said that he literally was a jester and Dulce was a Jackette. You became your role. And, that was where the first line of questions poured in.

To literally be your role, did that mean you weren't human? Or were you human with special abilities? How did all of that work? Tethering to the magic in a specific role, what and how many abilities you got, whether abilities were exclusive or if everyone had the same…

In the next tangent, aging. Theoretically, most of the carnies must've been from eras gone by. As in, eras dating to the last century and they did not reflect their real ages. A few questions came to mind with this topic, but it wasn't as prevalent as tethering and abilities.

And now thinking about it, Lement's younger brother Dennis has aged. He was two years younger than me. When I first started, he was a small pre-teen to turn around and become another towering Radu within a three-year window. He's also gone on to become the carnival's magician in that time. So somehow, he was part of the carnival but is still aging? What was the fine print to that?

Regardless, the topic of the Founders came in to play. As in, two of my favorite people worked for the magical carnival while my parents worked with the magical amusement park. What were those odds?

I bit my lips as the Ringmaster, *the real Ringmaster,* popped into mind again. His sayings about coincidence and purpose, his sayings about he's too good to be a part of my imagination. That did not sit well. That *really* did not sit well.

That curbed the rest of my thought processes and I sipped the steamed milk.

This was real and surreal at the same time.

With a deep sigh, I took another sip. A knock at my door drew my gaze. Lement peered in curiously.

"Might as well," I greeted with a grin.

Lement welcomed himself inside and slid into the booth on the opposite side.

"You're mulling." He leaned forward and planted his chin on his right fist. He bore a wicked smile.

I nodded and downed more steamed milk, "I was."

"Good," He replied, "Now, ask away."

I bit my lip as I contemplated what I wanted to ask first. Starting head on into the Founders and Cirque Arcana was well enough.

"Parlour Lane," He began, "Cirque Arcana?"

Lement's face held a peculiar look of amusement and exhaustion. The fact that the hubs didn't get along was the most simple, straightforward tidbit to come to light today.

"Parlour Lane," He mused, drumming his fingers against the table top, "You know how some people have these tragic backstories that made them become so terrible?"

I tilted my head.

"They're not those. They're the ones who were just born that way. That's all there is to it. They're old fashion, so you know, a healthy dose of subliminal misogyny, racism, narcissism… Horrible brood. Lame as hell, boring as hell, hateful as hell, fake as hell, power hungry…" He explained.

I couldn't help but chuckle, "There has to be some sort of redeeming quality?"

Lement snorted in amusement, "They're great to be around to people they like. But they tend to like birds of a feather."

"Right."

"And Cirque Arcana…" At the sound of the name, I died a little inside. He continued, "Well, you know Cirque Arcana. What do you want to know specifically?"

I let out a dry laugh, "What's his name?"

"Gabriel."

It took me a moment of silence before I could respond. I had to remind myself of his explanation as to why he never told me anything before.

"Is there anything else I should know about it?"

Lement paused as well, his eyebrows contracting together, "Ask him about Sabyne next time you see him."

"Who's Sabyne?" I asked, confused.

Lement smirked in response, "His wife."

The thought of someone loving him and him having the capability to love someone else was entertaining. She was probably as ridiculous as he was with a matching 'holier than thou' attitude. It made me snicker… and then think of an idea.

"Do you know where he is?" A better idea then formed, "Can you make things teleport?"

An inquisitive glean resided in Lement's pale yellow eyes, "Why?"

"I want to write him a letter and ask him about her now."

Lement guffawed at that and manifested a sheet of paper and pen out of thin air, "Tell him I said hi!"

I chortled in amusement as I tapped the pen against the table, "How come *you've* never sent him any love letters? Isn't that your specialty…pissing people off?"

Unexpectedly, Lement's enthusiasm subsided, "… he's who killed Mildred." My jaw fell, but he shook it off before I could say anything, "It's okay, I'm still in the process of creating hell for him as he has done. He'll love hearing, excuse me, reading my name. It will piss him off."

Once more, I bit my lip. It was probably a habit my lips were especially unappreciative of at this point.

"Good." Was all I knew what to say. I continued tapping the pen against the table top and then proceeded to the next line of thought. "He haunts my head, my parents work with the Founders, and you're one of my best friends." I mused, causing him to grimace. "What are your thoughts?"

Lement reclined back in the booth as he contemplated his response, "You've caught his eye, that's for sure. Odds are, you've caught the Founders' eyes too. Me, well, you applied here and work with me so that just happened. Maybe your parents have been working with the Founders for a long time and Gabriel caught wind of that, got curious." He then smiled wickedly, "You're a freakshow magnet, Nannette!"

"Do I at least get to enjoy it?" I quipped rhetorically.

Lement's smile intensified, "Oh, we're going to make it worth your while."

I had no doubt about that. Now that the cat was out of the bag, Lement and Briley and Dulce and the others would have a field day getting to showboat.

"Now," Lement gestured to the blank paper mischievously, "Write that letter."

SCENE TEN

Behind the carnival and the airstream park was the precious sliver of bare fields that remained untouched. That was where I found Lement, Dulce, Kellan, and Briley. The jester, the Jackette, Mayhem, and Trickster. They were standing around two erected metal poles. Stretched in-between them was a wide rope about six feet from the ground and about two inches wide. Lement seemed to be chiding Kellan, likely residual of yesterday. Briley and Dulce were playing on the poles.

As I approached my roguish crew, I tried to make out what they were bantering about, but my gaze kept reverting to the line. A small waft of the wind and the line shifted. Only those who lacked the sense of self-preservation would want to tight rope walk in this wind without any crash mats below. Enter the five of us with no senses of self-preservation at all. Then again, the other four probably didn't have to worry about what would happen if they fell. As for me though… six feet wasn't that high.

I held my arms out to the group and melodically beamed, "I'm so glad you all could attend," then, I spun around cheerfully, "to watch me bust my ass. You're all so kind."

Lement bowed, "Of course, my lady. But the day you can't walk a tight rope will be the day pigs fly."

"Is that so farfetched considering you can teleport?" I quipped.

A smirk drew on his face, "Fair point."

Briley grinned down from sitting on the pole he'd climbed. Dulce strolled over to me.

"We're not just tight rope walking, lovely." She hummed.

Lement interrupted, "That'd be too boring."

"We're going to teach you some magic." Dulce continued, a twinkle in her eye. "Teleporting and gravity defying."

Cue cheeky grin, "That would've been useful several days ago."

Lement matched my grin, "It would've been more useful if you told me what was going on before several days ago."

My middle finger saluted the jester when Dulce grabbed my hand and guided me to the pole Briley was still perched on. All the meanwhile, Kellan shifted to watching the rope shift in the breeze, paying the lot of us no mind.

"It's a matter of will." Apparently, Kellan was paying us mind after all, "You believe you can do it by magic. If it works, it's a talent. If not, it's not for you. Simple as that."

I grabbed the base of the pole just as Briley did a backflip overhead off of it. Lement pranced to join Dulce and me.

"That simple?" I was dubious.

"Why, sure," Lement chimed, "When you're at a faction. If you're out on the streets, you have to be tethered to magic to do magic. If you're here, you don't have to be tethered. You just have to try and see what you can and can't do. But the key part is believing it."

"Being of magic helps," Briley added, causing Lement to quickly look questioningly at him, "Like your brother, Lement," the Trickster added. "He's not tethered but he's second generation. It's an advantage. It's not to say other people can't though."

"Can we get started?" I cut to the chase. I was eager to play around with the lighter hearted aspects of magic. And regardless of how surreal and unnatural it still felt, learning it was still an exciting prospect. It was one more layer of confirmation that it was real; not just seeing it for myself but feeling it for myself.

Rather than being productive, Lement mimicked me in my own voice, "Can we get started?" He flicked back imaginary long hair.

My face frowned and I leaned into Dulce, "I don't like him."

"Just ignore him, baby doll." She whispered with a smile, "You know human flag?"

In the next second, Dulce grabbed the top and bottom of the pole with the palms of her hands facing away from her. She then twisted her torso as she raised her legs from the ground. Her body was parallel to the ground. She was holding herself perpendicular off of the pole with two hands.

"From there, it's easier to tuck in," she continued to explain and demonstrate.

She brought her knees to her chest and using her arm strength, pulled herself towards the pole so that her body curled in between her arms and her feet rested against the pole. Essentially, she was crouched on the pole horizontally in the same way someone would regularly crouch on the ground.

"And then you would just stand." Dulce pivoted her feet, so they were parallel with the pole and straightened up, so she was standing horizontally.

"Now, if you lost balance and fell, would you fall to the ground or…?" I inquired.

Dulce nodded, "If you lose balance, you stop defying gravity, therefore gravity takes back over and pulls you to the ground."

"She's cheating though," Lement piped up, "She's levitating, not defying gravity."

"It's the same look to show her, buttercup." With that, Dulce pushed off of the pole and hovered in the air, turning herself back up. She grinned as she returned to the ground.

I blinked, "Excellent."

I took a step forward before looking between Dulce, Lement, and Briley. Kellan stayed further back although he was watching.

"I've never done a human flag before." I forewarned.

Lement scoffed, "First time for everything, Nannette."

"I'm just saying, there's a good chance I'm about to break my neck."

"Damn, I didn't bring my phone to record." Briley gleamed, ruby eyes wild as ever.

Dulce pushed him aside. I prepared my grip on the pole as I thought over what it'd feel like to break my neck. Was it instantaneous death? Was it painful? Time to find out. Without hesitation, I hoisted a leg up.

Every fiber of my mind concentrated on ignoring gravity. This was possible. God knows, this was possible. With everything that the others had done, this was doable. Whether it'd be doable for me- it was. It needed to be. It was possible. I could do it.

Prudently, I lifted my left leg slowly. Initially, every muscle in my arms and abdomen exerted itself to keep myself aloft. A moment later, it ceased.

Lement and Briley spotted me as I judged how I felt. I was still vehemently concentrating on being lightweight, pretending gravity didn't exist. Walking up poles and walls were carnie casual.

I also assessed the change in initially lifting up to how I felt now. There wasn't a sparkly, happy go lucky feeling or anything else. But I did feel the weight shift from pulling to the ground to feel as if I were doing a handstand.

I was going to chance it.

I curled inwards into a crouch and stood up straight. Lement and Briley's hands caught my back at my sudden action, expecting me to fall. But I didn't.

It was like I was standing upright on the ground, all the same. I took a few steps forward, up? Both? I was balancing on the pole as if it were the tightrope. My eyes centered on the rope.

With steadier steps forward, I took a foot and planted it on the rope. Leaning my body back, I shifted my weight onto that foot before bringing the next foot onto the rope as well. I was standing upside down on the tightrope.

It didn't feel special. It didn't feel weird. It felt natural. It was no different than standing upright.

I tilted my head back to look at the three on the ground who were staring back at me with enthusiastic expressions.

"Lement, can you do this?"

He shook his head in response.

I grinned deviously, "You want to take me on that sling shot right now?"

"Sure, I'll teleport you there and the only way for you to escape the restraints is to see if you can teleport off it." He replied cheerily.

My happiness died, "Dulce, how do you teleport?" I was frantic.

"Dulce can't teleport. Only I can." He was enjoying my desperation, but offered, "You just will yourself."

My eyes flicked over to the platform on the opposite end of the tight rope. I could do this too. I just defied gravity, I could teleport. I needed to be able to teleport. Teleporting was easy. One place in one second, another place in the next. It was no problem. It was easy.

…

"I can't do it."

"Try harder, doll face!"

"I am!" I called back to Dulce.

Regardless of my willpower's intensity, it was not happening. Here I was still standing upside down on a tight rope, but I couldn't teleport. It wasn't for a lack of trying. So, it must've been something the magic decided wouldn't be useful for me. It didn't understand how badly I needed to escape the sling shot. Why did I remind Lement?

"Come back down, Nannette."

I looked skeptically at Lement, "Nah."

Dulce slung an arm around Lement's neck, "I won't let him take you on the sling shot." She promised, ignoring the sour look Lement shot her. She didn't notice Briley wink at Lement, however.

"Briley too!"

Dulce's brown eyes met rubies and bore them down until their owner ceded with a sheepish smile. I didn't worry about Kellan as he preferred torturing people verbally.

"Come on! We've got show and then I want to play some more at our venue." The Jackette said.

I didn't get down until I'd given both Lement and Briley pointed looks. Two smug smirks were my only response from them. I knew it was a matter of time before they carried out their scheme.

* * *

'Miss. Sinclair. Never mind your faux concerns in my personal affairs. I assure you the matter of your own is presently paramount. In the spirit of candor, your parents are vastly disheartened at the dearth of intellect you have inherited. Lemuel is preying upon this very vulnerability. The deception is clearly unambiguous to all but you and truthfully, you will meet fatal repercussions should you continue to entrust him. If you have the

slightest inclination for your mother's heart, see to it that there is a shred of self-preservation in place of intelligence.

Emcee'

It took little over a week for the Ringmaster to respond. For all I'd known, he hadn't gotten the letter or didn't care to write back. A part of me wondered if he'd just show up in my dreams again, but that never happened either. There was no answer until now.

It was refreshing to see he was as disparaging and insensitive as ever. Maybe I should be honored that he bothered to write me at all. That was probably a waste of his time. I might've pushed the right button, though, to peeve him enough to retort.

I simply stared at the letter. He hopped on the 'Lement is a terrible person' bandwagon, one that'd I'd never join. Quite frankly, I couldn't be bothered with how Lement acted to everyone else, what he's done, what the opinions of others are. He could be playing me for all I cared, but I didn't.

I had accepted the whole concept that was magic. I'd learned quite a bit by this point and came to enjoy it. Simply not caring about anything anymore solved the apprehension of its nature. It fixed the fact that I was caught up between three factions for some reason, two of which wanted my head. Let's just go ahead and add the third one to it.

Call me stupid, but in my newfound freedom I found myself growing increasingly indifferent. Whatever happened, happened. What was the point in troubling myself over it?

Dulce had mentioned that the more you embraced magic, the more it'd start to effect people even if they weren't tethered. They were still channeling magic, so it'd still heighten your good attributes and bad. And I could see it.

For starters, that explained Kellan. It explained how wild Lement and Briley were. It explained how free-spirited Dulce was.

For me, it was making me more shameless, fearless than before. I only noticed this difference on account of *I willingly rode the sling shot*. The very ride I hated with a passion, I turned around to 'meh, whatever.' It wasn't overnight, but it happened much to Lement and Briley's delight.

Surely, it'd make me more reckless too, but that was the way to live at a carnival. A magical carnival.

And regardless of what input anyone had to say, my friends were my friends. Our relationships were our relationships. Whatever anyone else had to say about them had no merit to me.

I chuckled at the letter and flipped it over to respond,

'Dear Gabriel, Emcee, Ringmaster,

The deception is clearly unambiguous to all but you if you think I care about my wellbeing. Neither sets of my parents did, and what does it matter if I die? Would ya miss me, Emcee?

Your favorite,

Estela'

With that, I stepped out of my airstream and back into the night. It was about an hour after midnight, which was fairly early to throw it in for the carnies, but everyone called it anyhow.

The string lights cast a warm glow that the reflected from the airstreams. I loved the atmosphere of it. It was especially rare in that it was quiet outside. Everyone had tucked into their airstreams for the night.

There was still a lingering eerie feeling that was particularly noticeable at night. Despite my newfound apathy, it nevertheless unsettled me. Fortunately, I found Lement's airstream soon enough.

I knocked on the door.

"Didn't we just say goodnight?" Came his whine from inside. He wasn't getting ready to sleep though. He was a night owl. This was only typical dramatic Lement.

"Can you send this to Gabriel before you kill me?"

He opened the door, intrigued, "Ooh, I'm killing you?"

He took the note and looked it over, impish grin never faltering. "Aw, he never said how. No sense of imagination." He remarked as he glanced at the back. With a flick of his wrist for effect, the note disappeared from his hand, "Message delivered."

"So, how are you going to kill me?" I quipped, humor on both of our faces.

Lement cocked his head, contemplating. His yellow eyes lit with curiosity, "I prefer driving people crazy. Sometimes, they do it themselves."

I snorted in amusement, "Good luck trying."

"Oh, I've never failed to succeed, Nannette." He assured wickedly.

* * *

Just a few miles from the carnival was a new shop that served alcohol infused ice cream, an ice cream barlour. And since we were sensible people, we were going to risk the excursion long enough to get some and find somewhere secluded to eat it before it melted. We being Dulce, Briley, Lement, and I.

We were all carpooling in Dulce's red Thunderbird. There wasn't another car in existence to represent her so perfectly. The wind agreed as it whipped through the open aired convertible.

I noted that some bit of sense did return to me when we'd left the carnival as I instantly second guessed how good of an idea it was for me to be riding along on this excursion. The fear of getting roped back to Melissa and Nick was back.

When I'd mentioned that at the time, Lement reasoned that no one would recognize me by a brief glimpse. After all, the police had shown up to the carnival looking for me. And seeing how I didn't even know that they were there, they couldn't have known that I was there. Suspected, but unconfirmed.

"We can go there." Dulce noted as we passed a playground nestled in the woods. Being a weekday, it was void of any children.

"Dibs on the slide!" Briley exclaimed.

I rolled my eyes, "You can't call dibs on a slide."

"But he did." Lement sided with the Jack. The jester was sitting in the back seat opposite of me. His back was leaned against the door and he fancied himself with laying his feet in my lap.

"It's okay," Dulce smiled at me in the rear view mirror, indigo hair flying in the wind, "We've got the swings."

Lement cackled, "But you didn't call dibs."

"You didn't call it." Briley confirmed.

"Then we call-"

"I call dibs on the swings," Lement cut the Jackette off, clearly proud of himself.

I glared at him.

"Who said I'm letting you back in my car when we get to the barlour?" She gave Lement a pointed look.

With a slight frown, "What choice will you have?"

"Simple," She grinned, "I'll light you on fire."

Another one of Dulce's talents was pyrokinesis. It was my favorite ability yet although I couldn't do it.

"Sure, you'll be lighting the wrong Lement on fire and I'll steal your car." He retorted. Another one of his talents was doubles. As if one Lement wasn't bad enough, he could make faux Lements appear.

"Or I could light all the Lements on fire."

I pushed Lement's feet from my lap, to which he replanted them back in place and crossed one over the other. I then recalled, "Yesterday you were just talking to Briley about not doing magic in public and here you are now."

"Damn it, Stela." It was the redhead, "Notice how I wasn't saying anything."

"Ah, ah, ah, children, children," Lement piped back up, "No one is to do magic in public… unless it's me. You can't fire me, you can't punish me, and if someone sees me, then I'll just kill them. Problem solved."

Lement was now engaged in humoring himself by satirizing the ill comments about him. With a smirk, I played along with Lement's sarcasm.

"I knew it was true!" I cried, "What Myrtle said, what the Ringmaster said. You're a lie!"

In response, he tipped an imaginary hat at me. Meanwhile Briley did what Briley did best. He flipped around in his seat and loomed over me,

"Shut up, you wench! You co-conspirator with this traitorous sorceress!" Briley then proceeded to pull a knife from his waist band and hold it back threateningly, "You must suffer."

"Sit," Lement, unexpectedly interceded, "Down. You're creating a scene."

"That's the point."

"We're supposed to be undercover, dipshit."

"Oh, yeah." Briley grinned as he sat back down in his seat. Lement laughed and playfully flicked the back of his head.

Par for the course.

SCENE ELEVEN

"That's tragic." Lement eyed Dulce and I judgingly.

We'd opted to share after seeing the inhumane portion sizes and great minds did think alike. There was no contest when we saw the cinnamon bun bowl stuffed with ice cream, bacon, and caramel. Whipped cream vodka was infused and poured over the top.

It also simplified this issue of me and my age. Briley had brought along Kellan's ID and a spare shirt so he was going to double as both since they looked similar enough, but Dulce and I knew there was no way we could tackle one on our own.

Lement and Briley weren't about to share ice cream as they wanted a whole heaping for themselves. How their taste buds and stomachs could handle such a rich mountain of sweets, I had no idea.

Coincidentally enough, they did get the same type of sundae and it was the sort of sundae that they did not need. It had an end all be all trifecta that was bound to have the same sort of chaotic effect as throwing a block of sodium into water. It was a waffle bowl with coffee ice cream, chocolate, and caramel whiskey. Sugar, caffeine, and alcohol. *Sugar, caffeine, and alcohol.*

"With your perfect bromance I'm surprised you guys didn't share," I retorted with a mouthful of cinnamon bun.

In response, Briley leaned closer into Lement, gawking at the jester's plate. With a split second mischievous smirk, Lement smashed his plate into Briley's face before stealing the latter's plate and resuming eating.

"Clowns," Dulce grinned to me as Briley guffawed.

"We're not clowns." Lement corrected bitterly.

"Yes, you are." I agreed with Dulce. Lement's yellow eyes narrowed at mine. I raised an eyebrow, daring him to do something.

"But excuse me," I corrected in a humored tone, shooting him a pointed look, "You're actually just a dumbass, scheming, manipulative liar who's probably outlived his natural life expectancy and yet still has only reached partial mental maturity."

Lement managed to choke on ice cream in laughter at my dig. Dulce lit up, "She burns better than I do."

"That was me being nice because he's still my best friend." I stated as Briley took on a mixture of amusement and shock underneath the smeared sundae on his face, "She knows?"

"Knows what?"

"What?"

The other three of us inquired, inquisitive. Dulce, Lement, and I shared the confusion of whether or not he managed to forget that I knew about magic. Dulce and Lement might've had an added layer of wondering what else he could possibly be talking about. For me, my other angle was whether or not there was something else I didn't know.

There couldn't have been. That just wasn't Lement. Sure, I was jesting about him not telling me about magic, but of course that wouldn't be something to just tell every person under the sun. God knows what the world would fall into if everyone had access to it. Not to mention, he didn't want to burden me with the unpleasantries that came with it.

Briley looked between the three of us trying to read the situation before he burst into a fit of laughter, rolling onto his back, and clutching his stomach. All the while, he licked everything on his face within vicinity of his mouth. This was clearly going to carry on for some time before he got himself back together.

"Maybe he's a clown." Lement noted.

I remained firm in my stance, fueled by caramel and bacon, "You're both clowns."

Lement pouted, "I'm not a clown!"

"Why do you take that as an insult?" I taunted.

"Because I'm a *jester* not a clown. There's a difference." Lement replied, matter of fact.

"What difference? The fact that they have to paint themselves up to look ridiculous?" Dulce let out an airy laugh, brown eyes filled with mirth.

Lement was still humorously unimpressed, "I'm going to ship you off to Gabriel. You can be his problem."

"Um, no you won't." Dulce corrected, "She's mine."

Briley finally managed to sober enough to rejoin the conversation, "So she *does* know about Gabriel?"

I snorted, "Well, duh. Where have you been?"

"Talking out his ass." Lement joked, throwing an arm around Briley's shoulders, and pulling him down into a casual headlock.

Dulce chuckled, "Because that's new."

"Because that's the way to be," Lement corrected, "Saying and doing stupid things is an underestimated power. It's the ability to make someone laugh if you want them to laugh or to piss them off if you want to piss them off. All while keeping a smile on your face."

Briley wiped the ice cream sundae off of his face and into his hands to eat what he had just been wearing. It was like watching a toddler in a high chair. Once his face was clear enough, he picked at the mashed sundae formerly owned by Lement.

"Girlie, we should ditch 'em." Dulce whispered, but kept her voice loud enough for the jester and Jack to hear.

"They're defecting," Briley leaned to Lement, whispering as well and also intentionally loud enough for us to hear.

"We're going to start a new faction." I leveled with the boys. Dulce happily agreed, "Yes!"

Lement scoffed, "And do what? There's already the theme park, carnival/sideshow, and circus."

"There's not a theater." Dulce replied smugly.

"Lame."

"Lame."

Both guys echoed, snickering. It was hard to believe they were adults. Then again, they weren't human. I rolled my eyes at them.

"Can you guys hurry up and finish so we can get back to the carnival. I don't want to get caught." I knew the chances were slim. What was the likelihood of cops riding by here in particular? And it was ridiculous to think that some stranger off the street might recognize me and call me in. But I still wanted to go back to the safety and nonchalance of the Midway.

"Aw, Nannette, you don't have to worry about your parents anymore. Relax." Lement eased, not at all concerned. Briley spoke up before I could speak.

"Who *would* you rather go back to? Nick and Melissa or Gabriel and Sabyne?" Briley grinned, the mischief clear as day.

It was apparent that the question was innocent enough. There was more to Gabriel that he knew and thought I knew too. He didn't realize the hell storm he'd just unleashed.

"What?" Lement scowled.

Briley's ruby eyes darted questioningly to Lement.

Dulce frowned at her troupe mate, "She can't go back to Gabriel, she can't control dreams like that."

"I've never met Sabyne." My face was far more balled up than Dulce's, in part confusion and sourness at the thought of willingly choosing to be with the Ringmaster and his wife.

Briley's wide eyes shot from Dulce to me and then to Lement. Out of reflex, he leaned further back and stammered, "Oh, damn, uh," an anxious chuckle escaped him, "I thought that was in real life. I didn't realize it was a dream. Sorry."

I didn't like my gut feeling. I *really* didn't like my gut feeling.

"That's it?" I questioned.

Lement snorted, "As I was saying about stupid things."

Dulce ran a hand down my back as I continued to glower, "Yeah, let's ditch 'em."

Patience and I still weren't good friends. Biting back my emotions was still an ongoing problem of mine. Would I rather go back to Nick and Melissa or Gabriel and Sabyne? Gee, what implication was that exactly? What was it the Ringmaster said about coincidences? Wasn't magic supposed to be the one bombshell? *The* one bombshell?

What anyone else had to say about how they acted around other people still didn't hold a single ounce of weight to me. They could be serial killers for all I cared. These were the people that were my family when I, pretty much always, had no real family.

I was on my feet. Dulce followed suit and replaced her hand on my back, "Come on, doll. We can finish this elsewhere."

"Why'd he ask that?" I breathed, my clear eyes locked on her browns.

She let out a sigh and quickly glanced at Lement. There was something there.

Without another word, I spun on my heel and came down off the playground. I felt numb inside, unsure of what to do.

Dulce followed me down as I could hear Lement shuffling and Briley cursing.

"Nannette!" Lement called, voice back to normal. The only ever time it was normal was when something serious was going on. It only solidified the cruel voice in the back of my mind.

"Stela, take the keys and get in the car. I'll talk to them." Dulce hummed, holding out the ring. I paused long enough to grab them from her and continue on away from the playground. The sound of two thuds into the mulch signaled Briley and Lement jumping over and off the railing. Try as she might, Dulce could try to talk Briley into giving me some time, but she wasn't going to be able to get Lement to listen. It didn't matter.

I hopped into the red Thunderbird into the driver's seat. In one fluid motion, I plugged the keys into the ignition and threw the car into reverse.

"Teleport home." I called out as three sets of surprised eyes landed on me. Before I shifted into drive, I gazed at them, filled with mixed emotions. I wanted to be wrong, but I knew I wasn't. As desperately as I wanted me to be jumping to conclusions, I had the foreboding feeling that I wasn't. I wanted to drive off a cliff.

"To answer your question, Briley…Nick and Melissa. At least death is honest." The Jack's face was still regretful for having dropped the ball, Dulce's was concerned, and Lement's was anguished. I didn't want to see any of it. Again, I wanted to drive off a cliff.

"Nannette, you can't!" Lement called back.

I put the car in drive and tore out of the playground parking lot and turned right onto the road into town, ignoring him. The steering wheel was unappreciative of the iron grip I had on it. It wasn't as unappreciative as my bottom lip.

The world felt surreal. There wasn't a single thing that felt real.

I pulled out my new phone to search for Cirque Arcana. Magic or not, the carnival still had guest service lines. As such, the circus did too.

Imagine the level of chagrin I felt as I saw their website popped up. For all these years, had I simply searched up the circus from my dreams, I'd have realized it was all real.

With a growl, I dialed the number and put the phone on speaker.

After a few rings, the box office associate answered. Hearing her voice only upset me further, "Stela Sinclair. Get me Gabriel."

"Miss- oh, okay. Let me see if he's available." The woman at the other end of the line pleasantly replied. The most innocent voice for the most horrid circus to exist.

"Tell him with any luck I'll be dead in the next day."

The lady didn't respond. Somehow gripping the steering wheel even tighter, the moment of silence from the other end played my nerves like a harp. I was apprehensive.

After a minute or so, I could hear the line reconnect. My grip tightened still yet.

"Miss. Sinclair-"

"Gabriel Sinclair, let me guess." I interrupt, voice filled with venom. The smug tone he started in sparked a fire.

I could feel the incense on the other end of the line. Likely not because of what I said, but because I cut him off. He was that type. *That* type. I felt like one of those stereotypical kettles from a cartoon ready to explode.

"I don't even know what to say. You're…" I couldn't even bring myself to say it, "And you killed my best friend's sister. Why do you even bother getting into my head at night? It's not like you care."

"How unforgiving is the world, is it not?" His voice was cold, "Do you truly believe Lemuel knowing now who you are to him? More concisely, what you are to him."

Incredulous, I shot back, "If there's one thing I believe, it's that you killed her."

Gabriel chuckled cruelly, "Why yes, Miss. Sinclair. I crushed her neck in my grasp, right in front of her brother even. And, I would not hesitate for the slightest moment to do it again."

It was impossible for me to bite my bottom lip any harder without drawing blood. Bad habit, I knew.

"She pursued a mission seeking death and death was what she found." He continued, "Nevertheless, disregard your pitiful distress of those matters. That is not what you are troubled with."

I ignored him, "I'm going home to the home you gave me."

"It is my understanding that is not in your best interest. Has Lemuel not informed you? Have you even considered that there might not be a home to return to on that front?" His voice was grave. He likely didn't like the notion of 'the Ringmaster's daughter' willingly going to do something stupid. He was like Melissa and Nick, it was how I reflected on the 'family.'

"My best interest would've been you just crushing my neck instead of shipping me off for someone else to do the job for you." Came my retort.

His distaste transcended the phone again, "You are not thinking rationally," His tone shifted, "Consider-"

"Best of luck on tapping into my dreams when I'm six feet under," I interrupted again, "That's where I plan to be within the next 24 hours."

"Estela-"

"'...spare your insincere distress of those matters,' *father*." My new phone then became the second phone of mine to fly out of a car and into oblivion.

* * *

I'd closed the roof of the Thunderbird once I'd gotten back into the car from an odd grocery store I stumbled upon. I had every intention on dropping back in on Melissa and Nick, but I figured that could wait until morning, bright and early.

There were only four days left until my birthday, the day that I thought I could finally escape. I'd go stay at a hotel somewhere long enough to get myself on my feet properly, simple enough. But here I was, already having escaped and now heading back to them. Who'd have thought?

I had driven aimlessly about throughout the city before just pulling into an outdoor outlet parking lot. There was a general store, so I went in and bought a bottle of melatonin with cash before taking twice over the recommended amount and crashing in the back seat.

I didn't want to be awake. I still don't want to be awake.

What was there for me to contemplate?

Take Myrtle up on her offer? For all I knew, she was Lement's collateral damage, part of a different faction, or an ex-carnie. I'd either be roping her into a mess or taking myself straight on into another one.

I considered reaching out to Rebekah, Aiden, and Cole but I faced the same dilemma of bringing an issue to them. Not to mention, I wasn't in the mood to find out that wasn't real either. Besides, I was fine. I didn't need to go running for someone. I was fine on my own. I'd been by myself all this time, I just hadn't known.

And to the Ringmaster's end, there wasn't much to note. From Briley's implication, Dulce and Lement's reactions, and Gabriel's own lack of denial meant that he could… very well be… my biological parent. It was asinine to consider. It would explain why he was in my head from time to time. But the other questions that could be explored with that weren't anything I cared about.

I never really gave much thought to finding my biological parents. I didn't think that would happen. And if it did, I didn't have any specific sort of feeling to gauge whether I would've gotten my hopes up or been hostile. Likely, I'd have been neutral and at best, hopeful they weren't like Melissa and Nick.

How ironic. They weren't like Melissa and Nick, they were worse.

I didn't want to be part of the Ringmaster.

I didn't know what I wanted anymore or what I was going to do. The latter was mainly a matter of why? What's the point?

Overreacting… underreacting… I was at a loss.

And I was awake.

I rolled over to grab my water and the bottle of melatonin off of the floor to fix that problem.

* * *

When my eyes reluctantly opened once more, the clock on the dash gladly enlightened me that it was nearly 5 o'clock in the morning, serenely oblivious to the nightmare situation. It must've been great to be a clock.

My heart wrenched and squeezed in pain. I had no direction. No clue what to do next. I had my life *somewhat* planned out before all of this. And somewhat was a strong word compared to the nothing of now.

The past week and a half wasn't a roller coaster, it was the zipper, a disorienting, chaotic monster.

I was spiraling, drowning… and going in an unending circle mentally. My mind simultaneously went too quick and was completely vacant at that same time.

Lement wanted to drive me insane? Perfect idea because it was killing me. Maybe going insane would've beaten the Founders to it.

One part of my head looped back to, I didn't need anyone. And then, no one needed me. It was a crippling cycle. I couldn't ask anyone how I should be handling this. Was I being ridiculous right now? I didn't like to dwell, as such, this was horrible.

But at the same time, everything felt so pointless. Was school the only closest thing to real I had? Was my life really only supposed to exist long enough to be collateral damage in some absurd fairytale episodic? For crying out loud-

Despite the resolve I had about my unlikely future, I fell off the backseat into the floor at the bump that rocked the Thunderbird. I hated startling easily with a passion. Have I mentioned that before? Here I was more than okay with the Founders doing God knows what to me and nonetheless, there I was in a ball on the floor.

I didn't dare move yet.

The anxious feeling in my chest kept me frozen, but my mind was screaming to just get out of the car and face whatever it was. It may have been something simple like a buggy blown into the bumper by the wind. It might be someone trying to steal the nice looking car. In one case, it was nothing. In the other, a jumpstart to getting put out of my misery might just be on the other side of a car door.

And even so, I stayed still, waiting to see if something else would happen.

Nothing.

…

Still nothing.

Cautiously, I climbed back onto the back seat and peered out of the back windows. The coast was clear. Or, so I'd thought until a soft voice spoke in a vintage accent, "You made this easy."

The pill bottle and water bottle were then tossed onto the seat next to me. I blankly stared at them with no particular thought in mind. I was back to numbness. But this time, the numbness was all there was.

I was fine with that. For once, I wasn't feeling an exhausting, contradictory concoction of emotions. It was just one simple one, numbness.

Without responding to the voice, I took even more melatonin.

SCENE TWELVE

By the third time my eyes opened after the latest round of melatonin, it was all I could do to keep them open. I was mildly surprised that they opened at all.

But there was one fortunate thing that I noticed right off the bat. I was at a faction. I knew it wasn't the Midway, I hoped it wasn't Cirque Arcana, and rationale told me that it was Parlour Lane. The voice I'd heard before going back under was an old fashioned, posh New York accent. The same type Sir and Lady had.

Of magic or not, they had to have real names. Sir and Lady was ridiculous.

So, Parlour Lane had to be the answer. And for whatever reason, I didn't consider that the reckless fearlessness would return once I was here since it was a hub of magic. It made things so much nicer. It brought a contented smile to my face.

It was all fine and well that they managed to find me within the half day that'd I'd been away from the carnival. Did they know I was headed for them? Or did they abduct me thinking that they accomplished some sort of feat? Did they feel special? Did they feel in control?

I grunted in amusement. Let them think so.

I had been moved into what looked like an office space. It was cleared out, boringly plain, but sized and located at a convenient spot that gave away what it was supposed to be.

There were two slits of old fashioned tinted windows rimmed with ornate white trim. I could look from the inside out but imagined people couldn't look from the outside in. There was no way they'd stick me away here if there was a risk that I could be seen.

Looking out of the window confirmed that I was in Parlour Lane Park. Now which Parlour Lane Park, that was another matter. They had half a dozen sprinkled across the country.

More specifically, I was in the 1880s section by the surrounding scenes. It was the front of the park, the first section you entered once you were past the ticket gates. At the far end from where you entered, the classic white wooden coaster lounged. The poor thing was old, so where as other coasters zipped about the track, this coaster took a lazy stroll. It still drew in the masses, nonetheless.

The area branched out on either side of the main street that shot down the span of this section. The architecture hearkened to a late 19th century town. As such, it was Greek Revival styled in tones of white, cream, and wood. Some of the awnings that were feeling a little bold donned burgundy coverings. There were path breaks between a few of the main street buildings for people to duck behind to other rides and eateries.

I couldn't recall which sections this one led into, at the moment. Not that it mattered much anyways.

Idly, I gazed out of the window.

There weren't people in the park. It wasn't open at the moment. But we were at the tail end of the week, yet. So, the crowds wouldn't pick up until the afternoon when people were getting out of school and work. Regardless, this was the only entertainment I was going to have for the foreseeable future until one of the Founders decided to grace me with their presence.

I then wondered if I could break the window. Did they have magic to protect it or was it vulnerable to whatever talents I could muster?

I took a step up onto the wall. Having done it before, it didn't take any intentional thoughts since I knew that I could do it. Hence, it was possible. No effort needed.

With my next step, I stood directly over the window. I knew that there was a good possibility that if it did break, I'd slip through it and back down to the ground. It'd be painful.

Despite that, I stomped my foot on the window. It didn't give. Then, I hopped on it several times. I tried throwing my weight and strength down through my legs to break it, but it still didn't budge. It rattled, unenthralled with what I was doing. But, it did nothing more than that.

Footsteps in the hall outside of the door climbed up a stairwell, bound for me. I decided to continue up the wall and onto the ceiling, sitting with a perfect view of the doorway. Upside down but still perfect.

The door was opened by what looked to be a security guard. He must've been standing on the other side to keep tabs on me, to make sure there wasn't anything amok happening in my holding room. In stepped three individuals.

Two were clearly Sir and Lady's kids, features being a blend of both parents. The third was an assistant of sorts. And despite being as such, he had a haughty, egotistical attitude about him. Surprisingly, the Founder duo struck as more apathetic than egotistical. Like the types to operate off of logic, void of empathy. It made me smirk.

"Gerald and Ruth Founder," The oh so special assistant announced, "Heirs of Parl-"

"Leave us, Kingsley." Ruth, an average height blonde whose soulless eyes were fixed on me, commanded their assistant.

He didn't look pleased to be so coldly dismissed in front of a guest, or should I say captive. He sat the cup and saucer he was carrying on the floor, exposing what appeared to be water. How kind of them.

Kingsley stepped out of the room. The security guard closed the door swiftly behind him.

"Is that real?" I grinned, eyes glancing over to where Kingsley had just left, "Does he really follow you guys around introducing you to people. Is he serious?"

Gerald and Ruth's faces changed none whatsoever.

"It's plexiglass." Ruth stated, referring to the window I'd tried and failed to break, "Bulletproof even."

We were cutting straight to the chase then. I was more than fine with that. It was my preference.

"So, how are we doing this?" I inquired.

Ruth blinked. Gerald's more lively blue eyes mulled over his answer.

"Drink." Ruth slid the saucer over with her foot while her brother thought.

My eyes flicked to the cup of water, but I didn't move.

Gerald's eyes met mine, "Give it a little while. Who's to say what could happen in the chaos? Three factions all at once? It hasn't happened for nearly 70 years."

His voice was the one I'd heard in the Thunderbird. He was the one to find me and bring me here.

"It hasn't," Ruth smiled a small smile, but you couldn't see it in her eyes. They were still empty, "Although last time it ended up in a mess. This one will clean up easily."

Gerald nodded his head, "Despite your thoughts about the carnival and circus, they are coming. You may not return the sentiments, but their sentiments are there. And once they arrive, we go forward to a new era together. Well, not everyone, but you understand. The death will have to happen by any means necessary."

I chuckled dryly, "So we're going to wait until they get here? If they *are* coming? We're going to bank on if they really do care? I wouldn't hold your breath."

"Both will come." Ruth assured, "But even if it's one, one will still be plenty to go forward with. That chaos, it's a very useful thing."

"Fine." I replied.

I cracked a sardonic grin, "I don't suppose Melissa and Nick will come running to my rescue?"

Gerald blinked apathetically, "Lemuel made sure of that."

Fantastic. Everything Gabriel and Myrtle had been saying about Lement's nature was true enough that my adoptive parents were likely dead. I couldn't be mad at that, though. It was justified. I shifted thoughts to a more pressing tangent.

I was the bait the Founders were using to lure out the carnival. They presumed that the Radus wanted their justice for Mildred's death.

And, I was the bait the Founders were using to lure out the circus. They presumed Gabriel wouldn't allow someone of his blood to stay pathetically captive by his enemy. How horribly that'd reflect on the perfect Gabriel Sinclair.

I was a two for one special. One bait, two factions. From there, heads would roll.

This was the calm before the storm.

Did calm really exist anymore in this point of my life? Is it suddenly going to exist just for the very end?

"Drink," Ruth insisted again, gesturing to the water, "You'll need it."

They turned and left the holding room without another word. With their exit, things would return back to nothing until *something* happened, whatever it was that they anticipated. How the factions fought each other had to be something of a game of chess with the various types of abilities in play. Why they fought each other was still a mystery.

Then again, I might not ever see it in action. The water could be very well poisoned by something or another. Imagine that. Lement and the Ringmaster come swooping into the rescue with the rest of their crews and save me just in time for me to choke on my own blood or something. It would be fitting. And admittedly, it would be funny. Stupidly funny.

I came down from the ceiling and took a seat in front of the cup and saucer.

Let it be poisoned, let me die. I didn't care.

I drank the water.

* * *

It was mind numbingly dull and uneventful for a while, several hours it felt like. I wished Gerald allowed me to keep the melatonin. But I suppose he wanted me conscious for the anticipated confrontation.

The air changed though. It was tense. I wasn't entirely sure how I knew without a doubt that whatever was about to happen was starting to happen, but I felt it. Unwaveringly, the storm was here.

I peeked outside of the windows again and it was still the same as it was earlier. Void. Beautiful, but void.

It was a deceptive sight.

I kept waiting for someone to appear, something to pop off, any sort of indication that this was it. But there was nothing visually. It was just in the air. The thick, uneasy air.

I turned back to face the empty cup and saucer on the floor, the most innocent thing on the property. Well, it was. Past tense, was.

Grabbing both, I walked up the wall next to the door and onto the ceiling just in front of it. With a hand, I held my hair back, so it didn't give me away.

I took the cup and saucer and beamed it at the floor underneath the window. Unceremoniously, it shattered with a loud crash. It was time to find out if the tension in the air was signaling something amok.

Sure enough, the security guard swung the door open. Presumably, and what I'd hoped for, he thought that I managed to somehow bust the window to escape. He'd thought wrong.

As he stepped inside to see the source of the noise, I dropped down into the doorway and exited the room. Before he could realize that it was a trick, I closed the door behind me, locking him in.

It was a gamble figuring that he was the only one out here to make sure I was in line. But I didn't have much of any other option.

I tore down the stairwell in a hurry before getting to the next door at the bottom. Surely, this was unlocked, but who could be on the other side? What was on the other side? Did it lead into the park? Did it lead into an employee break room? That'd be great.

Ever so incredibly gently, I pressed on the door. Thankfully, it wasn't noisy, but I still had to get it far enough open for me to see without it being too open for other people to see. It was a balancing act. I needed to give other people away without giving myself away.

I didn't have much of a plan anyhow, aside from getting to the center of the mayhem ensuing. I had a better chance of being safe in that room than going out into the crossfire where it was easier to get struck with a rogue throwing knife, or whatever it was they fought with. And, I didn't want to be safe.

Nevertheless, if one of the park people caught me right here and now, they'd just throw me back into the room. Hence, I needed to find a way to deal with them as I had the security guard.

I gazed in the crack to see what I could make out so far. It was quiet. That was promising.

What I could see was a wall similar to the ones currently surrounding me. It gave me the impression that it was another hall. Time to take the risk.

This door opened up to a corridor that led to a variety of different areas. To my front right, signs along the wall marked those two doors as being bathrooms. Further down to the right, the hall turned into another area. I could hear voices coming from that direction.

Along the left, there was another door with a small sign on it that I couldn't make out from where I stood. Across from where the hall turned right at the end, there was but another door. I knew I'd never know what it led to because it was too close to the voices for me to safely get to it.

As unbothered as I felt as of late, I wasn't stupid. Careless? Maybe. Flat out dumb? Not just yet.

Which reminded me, I was going to have to move on and as far away as possible from here quickly. The security guard that I'd locked into my holding room more than likely had a radio. Without a doubt he had called my escape in to the others. Maybe they'd be too distracted with which ever faction just touched down to focus on me. Then again, I was the bait for which ever faction. They needed me.

I quietly made my way to the first door on the left.

'EMPORIUM'

That was going to have to do. Ideally with the park closed, there wasn't going to be anyone inside of it. But then again, realistically, this was going to be a game of inevitably running into people that I'll need to handle so I can find where the action will be going down. And that was banking on if I could actually pull that off.

Attentively, I slipped behind the door into the Emporium, quick to catch the door behind me so it latched without noise. If anything, the people down the hall might figure it was other employees. But, I wasn't going to take the chance considering the circumstances right now.

The door entered into the shop from the back right corner, nestled between two display stands.

The Emporium was atypical of regular amusement park souvenirs. It was clearly the park's merch based on the branding, but the merchandise evidently varied based on the section you were in. A lot of the keepsakes in here were hand carved wooden figurines, toys, porcelains, candles, and décor.

Fortunately, it was void of anyone else at the moment. The unsettling feeling in the air was the storm setting in. But the Emporium didn't have any umbrellas. Now what it did have, however, was fireplace pokers at the hearth behind the checkout counter.

No one would be able to get close enough me to take me back to the holding room. Not to mention, because it was a weapon, the Parlour Lane folks had no choice but to take me down. Opportune timing would change from when it'd be the most perfect breaking point making the other factions watch me die, to having to kill me to avoid getting beaten with a poker.

To think, just two weeks ago was just another day in the life as the Sallows' child, horrible, looking forward to the next two weeks in which I'd be free. I was never free. I was a blind fly sitting in a spider web without any idea. This was all inevitable.

There was nothing else to lose now. I wasn't going to go back to the holding room. I wasn't going to go back to Melissa and Nick's. I sure as anything wasn't going to go back to the carnival. And what was I going to do? Go 'back,' I guess, to the circus?

Death was definitely more appealing.

Giving the poker a twirl, I headed out the front of the Emporium on to the park's main street area. I needed to find where the action was. It was silent to the point that if it weren't for the sensation in the air, I'd have sworn that the whole property was a ghost town. But, it wasn't.

I spared a glance off to the left, where the entry gates were. That, too, was empty. There wasn't as so much as a security guard there.

Looking to the right, the coaster resided. It was freshly painted and clearly kept up well, but that didn't hide its age. Maybe it was because of the Founders. Lement said they were superficial people. Ruth and Gerald were certainly callous people. And the whole park reflected that. For as beautiful and polished it was, it felt artificial. It felt fake.

I barely took a step towards the coaster to head farther into the park when movement from the lift caught my eye.

There was someone standing on top of the lift. Whoever it was, they were more ghastly white than the coaster itself and anything else I'd ever seen. It simply stood still, facing me.

It then dawned on me; the attractions at the carnival had a sentience about them. The ones here likely did too. And the ones here, seemed to be on a different level if the person on the coaster was a manifestation of it.

I chuckled humorously at the irony. Maybe I didn't need to make it to the thick of the action. I hadn't considered the rides along the way.

Wordlessly, the figure continued motionless. It wasn't there when I'd first looked at the roller coaster. So, whoever, whatever it was on the lift was in response to me walking out. It just hadn't done anything else yet.

I continued to watch it, presuming it was watching me as well.

Wisps of abnormally white hair floated, or at least I supposed it was hair. The wind carried it ever so slightly in the breeze, but it continued to hover around the head instead of fall back down as gravity would have it.

With a snort, I took another step out of curiosity.

I wasn't fully expecting the deafening banshee shrieks that the being proceeded to emit. It was impressive, really. The lungs on the thing. It was the most piercing, and undoubtedly inhumane sound I'd ever heard. And it was still screeching. It didn't stop. Not for a second, not to catch its breath.

My ears would probably be bleeding in another minute or so if it continued in its screams. It still stood like a statue but shrieked as if it was in agony. It was one continuous, haunting call. There was no way the rest of the nearby cities couldn't hear it.

Mildly in a sort of bewildered awe, I took one more step.

The figure kept endlessly screeching, not faltering for a moment. But, it then began to rapidly descend the lattice support structure in a swift crawl.

It was on the move.

It was headed for me.

Even if I'd chickened out and decided to run, there wasn't a person on the planet capable of outrunning the thing. Magic or not, it was on a mission.

It only took a matter of maybe ten to fifteen seconds for it to clear the distance down and to me from where it'd been about eighty feet up in the air, 100 meters away. Again, it was impressive.

My grip tightened on the fireplace poker in anticipation. And then blood flew.

SCENE THIRTEEN

The blood was cold, colder than ice. You'd think by now, I'd get used to how unnatural so much of everything was. But, no. It still managed to catch me off guard.

Blood wasn't supposed to be cold. It was supposed to be warm.

My feet were drenched in the pool of blood. Splatters covered my front side entirely. It was on my lips, but I didn't want to taste it. That wasn't the last thing I wanted to taste in my tragic existence.

The desolate stillness was gone. It managed to die before me. I was mildly envious.

The call of the coaster being summoned every living soul in the park. The rest of its own Parlour Lane must've known I was the source of why it screamed. And any of the other faction members from Cirque Arcana and The Midway that were here, must've followed after them. Likely, they had a pretty good idea at what would cause the whole park to move in on the main street.

Flying down from the building roof tops were mass swarms of freakshow personnel, from performers to the stage crew. Those on foot from the ground crashed through shop windows and hurdled turnstiles to pour into the street.

I was perfectly content with this being the last thing I saw. It was sheer chaos. It was beautiful.

The blood, the illusions, the fire, the shape shifting, the strength, the pyrotechnics… some of the sights before me, I don't even know how to describe them.

Someone who looked to be a technician pulled a two way radio from his belt and hurled it into the fold. The radio turned out to be a bomb, like an inconspicuously dressed grenade. A magician telekinetically flung it back into the air where it blew out the second floor of a café.

The clowns, that I recognized from Cirque Arcana, proved to be cannibals. Or at the very least, they didn't mind the taste of flesh as they tore out the necks of anyone they could get their hands on like rabid animals, all while laughing maniacally.

There was a being entirely made of water, with no distinguishing features, circling the crowd. It was shifting forms to easily sweep enemies off of their feet and trying to drown them. It darted off after getting lit up and nearly evaporated from a pyrokinetic.

An acrobat ran up a wall to flip off backwards and land on a stagehand before twisting the latter's neck around in a perfect 360, nearly severing the head completely.

Flaming arrows littered the sky, as did fireworks that singed anyone within range.

Contortionists might as well have been a bar of soap. No one could get a proper grip or hit on them the way their bodies were seemingly made of elastic.

The second I heard a chainsaw roaring to life, I knew it was Briley.

Ruth and Gerald had been right. Both of the other factions showed up. It made me wonder if they were all fighting each other or if they came to fight the Founders specifically.

And here it all was.

Not a single one of them likely cared about me, who I was as a person and my wellbeing. But because of what I was to them, a pawn, leverage, payback, here they all were in a scene of insanity.

They were all fighting because of me.

No one cared about me. I didn't care about myself. But still, I somehow managed to be the source for a brutal battle between the factions.

Like I said, maybe I should be used to the strange by now. But I wasn't.

Who would ever believe that within the matter of two weeks, *three powerhouses of dark magic* would be duking it out to stake their claim, their ownership of me? It was absurd.

But the madness of it all was breathtaking to me. I couldn't help but to be in awe.

Focus. I needed to focus. It was too easy to get distracted.

Collecting myself, I pulled the fireplace poker out of the head of the coaster banshee. It was still pouring freezing blood onto the ground at my feet. The scarlet was a stark contrast against its ghostly appearance and had dyed the white hair red. My ears appreciated the silence of its screeches.

The air was filled with a concoction of turbulent noise. But one sound couldn't be properly distinguished from another. It was a chorus of chaos. It was far less painful to listen to than the coaster.

I proceed forward down the main street towards the coaster attraction, dragging the corpse of its manifestation along by its blood matted hair. Would the ride itself still be able to run now that it, whatever the part of it was that I carried, was dead?

The thick of the havoc carried on through the end of the park section. The front part consisted of the select few who tried to come for me from behind but were met with circus and carnival performers. The bulk of everyone else was tied up between the coaster and me.

I had a better chance of getting struck by a rogue, flaming arrow going this way. And with the mutilated coaster being in my one hand and the bloody poker in the other, I had the perfect fuel to incite every Parlour Lane person to exist. It was only a matter of time of when the inevitable would greet me, not if.

Entering into the brunt of the mayhem, my eyes locked onto an identical copy of my own. Immediately, I knew it was Sabyne.

My eye color was closer to Gabriel's, but the shape was Sabyne's. My face structure and my lips were also unquestioningly from her. My nose and cheekbones were closer to her husband's.

Her hair was a light caramel color, seamless to her skin tone. Both features I inherited from her as well.

Briefly, the one thing that struck me was the most positive note to come from this whole situation. For society's flaws regarding diversity, circus has always been different. The same could be said for the carnivals. What country, hair type, skin color, religious beliefs, gender, orientation- none of that mattered.

So, with the age of the three factions dating back to times when race, religion, gender, and orientation were problematic; that was the one redeeming factor about them. They didn't care about a person's demographics, just whether or not they were talented at performing and at killing.

A flood of emotions lit her eyes as she gazed into mine. I kind of scoffed, blinked, and broke contact. I wasn't interested in this right now.

I continued forward with the coaster corpse in tow. So far, I wasn't getting struck by anything. Factions of all sorts were right around me, within an arm's reach and even a hair length apart at times. But, none of them paid me any mind.

It was like an illusion. They couldn't see me.

Just behind the roller coaster, a ballroom topped ever so slightly over head of it. Or namely, should I say, a few of the Moorish towers that decorated the roof did. Each tower was big enough to hold room for storage or maybe small private events, but it was clearly not accessible to the public. It was a perfect vantage point to see the chaos along the main street while being conveniently tucked away by the coaster.

Fittingly enough, the ballroom wasn't a new addition to hearken back to an older era. It was built in said older era as a then current, popular attraction. Now, it was the type of which to be an icon of that era, the same as a massive steel roller coaster represented this current one.

The Founders were an old fashioned people. They were in tune with the mentality that men took care of things and ran the household, while the women and kids were subservient. As such, Sir was somewhere spearheading the Parlour Lane's part in this battle royale, while Lady and their two heirs would be tucked away somewhere 'safe.' Kind of like a ballroom Moorish tower.

It was a perfect view, perfect distance. People would first think that they'd hide away somewhere in a bunker off property. It'd seem stupid to hide right at the front, center of the park. But there was safety in people overthinking. People wouldn't consider the ballroom necessarily because it struck as too risky and flat out stupid of a spot.

They could watch the chaos, relay information back to Sir even. But, they couldn't see into the chaos. Collective madness is collective. There wasn't any discerning of the particulars of what was happening. Everything was happening all at once, too fast for coherency.

And it helped, that no one else was seeing me. Sabyne managed to see me. But those on the ground next to me, they couldn't. I was hidden.

That meant, Lady, Ruth, and Gerald wouldn't see me wandering through just yet. But I was going to need them to. No one else was going to get the job done, but Sir and Lady. They needed to see me because they wouldn't hesitate now to just get it over with.

The effect of killing me would be beneficial for them in every way. It was the whole reason why I was here. They surely knew that I'd escaped the holding cell, but they probably erroneously assumed that I was trying to seek safety.

I wasn't seeking safety, I was seeking death.

I didn't need to press any buttons to get just one of the three likely in the ballroom to come down for me, but it wouldn't hurt just to seal the deal.

I could hear the Ringmaster's voice in the letter he'd written back to me, *'the slightest inclination for your mother's heart,'* he'd said, *'see to it that there is a shred of self-preservation in place of intelligence.'*

He didn't know me. Sabyne didn't know me. No one knew me.

It was bold to assume.

Reaching the outer skirts of the skirmish, I turned back around to face it. There was a trail of blood that led up to where I stood. No one noticed it, no one noticed me. The chaos continued in a stunning display.

See me.

I needed them to see me. How many people wanted my head and they were all missing it right in front of their faces.

A hand shot out from behind me and covered my mouth while another wrapped around my waist and pulled me back. Just like that, everyone could see me again. Whatever delusion that had hidden me before had been shattered.

I threw the coaster's maimed body down to my right, freeing my hand. I had no doubt it was a Founder, having gotten a good view of me from their perch atop the ballroom. I pressed the right button. This was finally it, all according to plan.

I couldn't have been happier, prey in the predator's grip.

Wicked ruby eyes gleamed as in the mayhem, Mayhem watched. Kellan smirked. He couldn't see the smirk I returned to him, but he knew.

With my other hand, I jammed the end of the poker stick down, causing my captor to double over. This gave me the perfect chance to run up the back of the closest person in front of me.

Whether it was a magician, another Jack, some other maniacal freakshow character, only God knew; but as my weight shifted from pulling down to earth to the back of my new 'ground,' the Founder lost what little of their grip they had left on me.

I pivoted on my platform's back and sprung forward to tackle who'd caught a hold of me. It was Ruth.

Don't get me wrong, I wasn't going to kill her. I didn't even have any intentions of hurting her. This was only a play, me setting up a false impression. I was adding a dramatic, theatrical flair to the death of an adoptive child seeking independence from an abusive homelife. Said girl who worked at a carnival, who's best friends were a jester, a Jackette, and a soft-spoken redhead from school. A girl who nearly made it to eighteen before her life went up in a spectacle of magic and mess.

That girl was about to die. She was broken. She was in the process of dying. And she found it the funniest thing in her life. Chalk it up to her dark sense of humor, her one final laugh.

I brought the fireplace poker down, squared in on Ruth's head, just between her empty blue eyes.

But, a grip on my hair jolted me off of the woman.

In the midst of it all, I could hear a woman's voice. I couldn't make out what it was saying, but I felt it. I knew it was my mother, Sabyne. She knew this was it.

This was it for me. It was all coming to a head.

I smiled.

I twisted up to be able to look death in the eyes. Lady.

Lady's typically composed, condescending eyes flared at me. And, then sharp metal pierced through the skin and sank in eagerly, tearing apart flesh to release a cascade of blood.

I went cold, numb, almost tingling. This was what ice must have felt like. Empty and frigid, but content. Euphoric.

The metal twisted, and the cold sensation intensified. It was almost addicting.

I knew the focus of anyone within the immediate vicinity of me and Lady had shifted to the two of us. But it was nothing to me. It didn't exist.

It was just Lady, me, the blood, and the cold.

Time had slowed. My focus was honed into Lady's eyes as they heatedly bore into mine.

My heart lurched, the only physical reaction I could discern aside from the tingling ice that encompassed me.

I let out a breath. It was a sort of sigh, a happy sigh.

It was done.

Finally, it was done.

* * *

Everyone had their own beliefs as to what laid on the other side of death. Whether or not souls were real, and where they went afterwards.

As for me, personally, I believed in God and Jesus. I imagined the lot of the circus factions were innately doomed on account of magic and the sick way it turned most of everyone who was tethered and born into it.

Whether there was salvation despite the inherent wickedness that came with it, we could hope. I did hope. I couldn't make any promises on being better going forward. Conquering my mistakes. Likely, they'd hold me down. They were engraved into my DNA.

Maybe I could do better one day if I weren't already too late. Hopefully, none of us were too late. I mean, we did have plenty of time to get ourselves together. It was just a matter of if we ever did. How long would that take? With as long as we have, would it not be enough?

These thoughts linger up until the very moment you find out.

* * *

The ballroom had the classical look and Moorish towers fitting of the late 19th century architecture, but the inside was a little more modern. Just a little.

The interior segued into an art deco style. The next section past the first one was themed to the roaring twenties. So, I supposed that it was meant to be a sort of juncture between the two.

The ceiling shot up to the roof two stories high and the walls were lined with plenty of windows for immense natural lighting. Pillars and arches supported the structure and hung chandelier lights for the night. At the far end of the entrance was the stage where a gorgeous ceramic mosaic completed the geometric, streamlined designed.

The ivory, cream, and black color scheme with gold accents honed it as a sight to behold. But, it wasn't as lovely a sight as the three factions' cease fire.

As beautiful as the chaos was, I fancied how these old, psychotic, wicked beings managed to be at a loss for words.

You'd think they'd seen everything at this point. There was no way anything could *truly* surprise them by now. Look at what they were. Look at what they did. How do you surprise them at this point?

The slight appall was entertaining.

"It wouldn't have been as effective sending letters out." Ruth said into a retro microphone. It was projecting her voice out to speakers outside of the ballroom so the many faction members could hear from where they were.

Gabriel was at the ballroom's entrance on the opposite side. He leaned against the doorway, face blank and unimpressed if anything. Sabyne stood just behind him, he wasn't letting her forward. The shadows concealed how she must've been feeling.

Lement, Briley, Kellan, and Dulce were just in front of the stage in the floor space. Lement had his arms crossed and face creased, Dulce was concerned, Briley was as aloof as ever, and Kellan sat on a table top with a cigarette. Classically, he couldn't have been bothered by the circumstance.

Remarkably enough, not one of them were disheveled by the previous epic. For all I knew, the Ringmaster didn't delve into the heat of it. But even the others who I knew were there, they appeared fine.

"And even to tell you in person wouldn't have the same effect." Ruth continued. Gerald stood next to her with two guys, street performers, donned in '50s fashion standing on the floor in front of him.

I leaned against the mosaic backdrop behind them, mirroring the Ringmaster. It was something only he'd notice, although he didn't show it, and I liked to think that it irritated him ever so slightly.

"We felt this would convey better."

The little bit of the ballroom's dance floor between the street performers and the carnie four was separated by Sir Founder. He lied motionlessly on the floor, bleeding from a bullet hole to the back of his head. It was a boring, quick event, but I guess Gerald figured the message was already taken by then.

Lement's pale yellow eyes never wandered away from me. He was trying to figure what to make of the latest turn of events.

Sir Founder was dead. Lady Founder was dead. Gerald killed one. I killed the other.

And here the three of us stood, and then the rest of them who pretended to care about me watched from the ballroom floor.

The look the jester was met with probably showed what I felt quite plainly. I didn't know what to make of him. I was still confident that he'd never cared about me and that I was payback, conveniently dropping into his lap. Vengeance for Mildred.

From the look in his eye, I liked to think that that wasn't the case. But I didn't trust him. I didn't trust anyone.

To that end, I was actually pretty surprised Myrtle hadn't shown her face yet. Whatever my relationship between Rebekah, Cole, and Aidan was, the one I had with Myrtle had always been fake. She was a doll. Literally, she was a living doll that Gabriel had planted to keep tabs on me when he wasn't in my head.

Everything about my life was fake. Including me.

Dulce glanced to Lement, wondering if he was going to say something. When he didn't, she opted to instead.

"What was all of this?" Her alto voice was tense. As liltingly sultry as it was, it was on edge.

I couldn't help but chuckle, "It's just champagne, baby doll."

"The ushering of a new era." Gerald paid me no mind. His voice was loud enough to carry over to the microphone.

The bulk of what I had to say, I didn't care whether people outside could hear it or not. The few that I did want to hear it were inside, right here.

I took a step forward, arms crossed, and casually meandered to the front of the stage, "To make me safe, you opted to throw me into hiding," I spoke to Gabriel and Sabyne, the latter of whom moved forward despite Gabriel's preferences, "When you could've dealt with these two."

I gestured to Sir's body, "But you're old fashioned."

Gerald gazed down at his father's body, "There's a weak way of handling things because of that. There's also a ridiculous mindset that comes with it too."

The sourness in his voice seemed to be aimed more so at his parents than mine, "The 'that's just the way it is' mentality." Gerald continued, "It's a threat to progress."

Ruth's head turned towards her brother as she smiled, "You all have done things a certain way for so long, we're changing that. And the only way to evoke dramatic change is to be dramatic."

I bit my lip as I glanced back to Dulce, Lement, and Briley before looking back at Gabriel and Sabyne, "Your intellectually disappointing daughter was doing what you couldn't and has now saved you from having to do anything else stupid for fear of safety."

Gabriel's lips curled up, "It was not on account of your safety, Miss. Sinclair. You proved yourself to be an inconvenience."

"Gabriel!" Sabyne hissed, though her husband paid her no mind.

Lement cut in with the most sarcastic chuckle, "Then what do you give two shits what I've ever had to do with her?"

Gabriel's grey eyes shot to Lement, a fire hidden behind them, "Your sister learned the cost of intervening in affairs that are of no one else's concerns."

My eyes narrowed, "You know I would've preferred she'd have just killed your wife. It would've spared her family and it would've spared me. You know, it would've spared you too, the inconvenience of me."

Both Lement and Gabriel's eyes landed on me. I guessed there was some part of the girl who was friends with a jester that didn't die. My eyes turned to Ruth and Gerald who were idly entertaining the exchange. They knew I had to sort the carnival and circus out enough that they understood the page we all needed to be on.

Despite Gabriel being Gabriel, who couldn't help himself with the callous slights, I knew both of my biological parents cared about me and that was why they gave me up. The amusement park and carnival factions didn't know I existed. Over a few years, I did prove myself to be a handful, so they reasoned it'd be better that I was passed off as any other kid, so I wasn't in the crossfires of the factions.

They'd tried to illusion me into forgetting that when I was little, but I never forgot. I always knew who the Ringmaster was in my dreams.

Melissa and Nick coming to work with the Founders was by no coincidence. I was the one to throw that idea out there, back when I played the part of their perfect little girl.

I knew what I was doing when I decided to drop that act and then sign on to work at the carnival. I knew Lement didn't know who I was initially, but I always knew who he was.

Lady and Sir Founder had never met me until two weeks ago, but Ruth and Gerald knew who I was. The three of us had always been on the same page.

Their parents were problematic, my parents' way of dealing with things was problematic, and the carnival held a strong potential of being problematic considering the factions' history.

How does that get resolved?

Ride out the circus' intentions over the years. In other words, if Gabriel wanted to think I was an oblivious, innocent child, then I'd be an oblivious, innocent child. To boot, I'd make Myrtle think the same.

I'd get Melissa and Nick to approach the Founders and sign on with them. It created a relationship between the two, a dynamic. Right around the time that I stopped being Melissa and Nick's perfect child, casually mentioning a few times the circus dream.

Then over time, once a rapport was built between the Sallows and the Founders, maybe the topic of a circus would come up. The carnival clearly did between the two of them. Then, the Founders would hear about my dreams and Gabriel's interest in me. Then, Ruth and Gerald would allude to me maybe being his kid. After all, I did look a lot like my mother when comparing the two of us.

With the circus and the amusement park on the hook, then it would be time to rope in the carnival. Let me work there, be who I'd probably be had I not been in the middle of such a colossal muddle. I could make friends easily. I could befriend anyone and everyone at the carnival. Then, there's a rapport between them and myself. Then, there's my insight on the carnival from having lived in its inner workings.

All of that tied together, eliminate Sir and Lady. Do so in a way that it doesn't get across the other two factions, but it permeates. The old mess of things was going to get cleaned up by the second generation of magic.

Sir and Lady weren't bound by emotion and were too caught up in their way of thinking that practicality and reason didn't resonate with them anymore. Gabriel and Sabyne were emotionally invested, so they'd follow suit as much as Gabriel was headstrong and arrogant.

The Radus had an emotional factor into play as well for the same results. And while their ties weren't as solid, reason came into play too. I knew them, how their carnival worked, the circus had devastated them before, and now the amusement park would be in the same line with the circus. They didn't have much of a choice.

It all wrapped up nicely. Everyone would coincide and everyone would know their place.

Magic did lack a moral compass. It did accentuate the best and worst in people. The best of all, it turned people into beings that weren't human.

My parents were human and had I been born when they were still human, I would've inherited who they were before they tethered. But they had me afterwards, I never had human DNA in me. I was second generation magic.

So, the genes I pulled from them, were who they are now. Cold, cunning, calculating, too confident, lacking empathy, unnaturally strong, capable of defying gravity, masters of creating illusions… the Estela they knew was who she would've been before magic. But she was born after magic, so the Estela they actually have is one who is a perfect storm of their immorality.

I smiled a jovial smile before Lement or Gabriel could respond, Sabyne's face was solemn, "This is out with the old, in with the new. Get on board or get run over, your choice." This made me laugh at myself, "Excuse me, I guess it's not much of a choice."

Gabriel's jaw subtly tightened. I could tell he was starting to hear himself, his cold inflection in my voice. My true lack of humanity. It was like when a mad scientist realized the monster they created but didn't want to accept it. They liked to believe they were still in control. He could try.

"We're going in a more assertive direction." I continued to explain, "Each faction's attraction needs a refresh. What was groundbreaking once is stale now. Cannibalistic clowns are not the worst things in the world. Driving people crazy is more of an artform than you make it. Most of you are people who became of magic. The part of you that was ever human hampers the potentials. Those of us who have always been magic, we don't have that flaw."

Ruth's smile grew and Gerald's chin tilted up, "We're graciously accepting our inheritance, in other words. This is the second generation taking the place of the first. *We* coincide. Should *you* create an issue, then you're done. We're not each other's nightmare, we are *the* nightmare. And you're all positively wholesome in comparison to the new reign we will create."

The inflection in his voice fully exhibited the nature of the psychopathic scheme underway. Dennis being the only exception, the few second generation magics there were proved to be more wicked than their parents. Dennis had to have it in him, somewhere.

I gestured to Sir's body, "Accept it or accept death."

The air was pin drop silent as my words sank in. Everyone outside likely turned into a state of disarray. Here things had been as they liked it, or better yet, as they tolerated it and now it was being shattered whether they liked it or not. They needed to adapt to the new status quo now or their future no longer existed.

Kellan, *Kellan,* began to laugh. He stood up, clapping, and flung the cigarette to the ground before putting it out.

"Finally," He smirked, "There it is."

Lement's murky eyes simply gazed at the Jack. Briley held a similar expression as he watched his brother.

Kellan grinned at me cruelly, "Finally." He repeated, sticking his hands into his pocket.

I snorted, "I still hate you."

Kellan's grin fell, "Well, no shit. Feeling's mutual."

I was glad we were still on the same page.

Sabyne eased forward, her face held an array of emotions, "I'm proud of your sense." She nodded, "I wouldn't expect anything less... You're our daughter, not our ally. We will never be your ally. So, whatever plan it is, we'll take as a suggestion."

The sternness in her voice made me smirk. She was a force to be reckoned with. There was no doubt about it.

"Would you kill me if it came to that?" I was curious.

Sabyne's eyebrows knitted together, but only in a sense that she was intrigued that I didn't know the answer.

"We will humble you."

She then took steps retreating back to Gabriel, who held a smirk of his own.

"Lemuel?" Ruth proceeded, keeping the conversation on track.

"Oh, I can't wait to see," he sang in his jester accent. He was concealing his true feelings.

I didn't like the part of me that wanted the carnival to agree to the terms. That part of me wanted them to agree because I missed them. That aspect was never intentional, but here it was. I didn't want to lose them, like I ever even had them.

The idea was to hook the Radus and friends on me, make them attached to me. Then, it'd be easier for me to manipulate their faction. But, they managed to sink a hook into me too. The part of Gabriel in me ridiculed it as being ridiculous, because now it was affecting me. I was caring about people who didn't care about me. I needed to remember that fact.

It was what it was.

While they showed up to Parlour Lane on my behalf, sure, it could mean that they might hold some sort of feeling towards me to tolerate Gabriel despite their history. But, at the same time they could be playing a long game of chess too. Trying to regain my trust to build our relationship back up. At that point of which, pull the rug out from under me in the years to come.

My heart ached.

Ruth and Gerald accepted his answer, all of our attention turned back to Gabriel. While Sabyne gave an idea, there was something more concise to be said from them.

Gabriel watched me, apparently content with answering on his own time. He was difficult to read sometimes. He was good at that, concealing. It was slightly maddening how unreadable he could be at obnoxious times like this. I knew deep down, he probably enjoyed it.

I stared back at him expectantly. Everyone did, except Lement.

I thought of my most recent dream with him, talking about the acrobats. My mother was evidence of this, they weren't known for their patience. That's where I inherited that too.

Gabriel smirked once more, knowingly. It was an unsettling knowingly that I didn't like.

Of course, he had to be my biological father.

"'...as you have decided upon acting out, my dear, I have found a newfound fancy of allowing you to make a fool of yourself,'" he quoted himself from the very dream I had just recalled.

He'd known.

"'...think, Estela, *think*. I know you have it in you.'"

ACKNOWLEDGEMENTS

I really don't know how to properly say thank you. Masqueraded has been a concept that I've tinkered with since 2014 before deciding to move forward with it as a whole deal of its own. And along the way, so many people have helped carry this story through. I don't think I'll be able to put it in words properly.

To my mom, Mary, oh dear. You already know reading this what this is going to be and how horribly I'm going to put it. Sorry! Haha. Let this whole project be a representation of you. My writing stemmed from you, the English teacher. You nurtured it my entire life. You've supported everything I've ever done my entire life. Sometimes that was being the first person at the gate when my circus troupe paraded out, racing from helping me change backstage to the audience to catch when I went on thirty seconds later, and championing this project from the very second I thought about it. You were left on cliff hangers as I was working along, you were following me up through editing and plot/character development, and your input when I was at a block has helped shape this story as much as I have. There hasn't been a second of my life that you haven't been both my biggest supporter and my biggest inspiration. I love you to pieces!

To my dad, Steve, Addy, by the time you're reading this point, think about how proud you are right now. You can't even begin to say how proud you are right? I'm every bit as proud of you as you are of me. Truly, I'm not sure you'll ever know just how much. You gave me your sense of passion, your entrepreneurial, and continuously give me security. I can turn around at any second and know you are there. I hope you know that at any time you turn around, I'll be there. That's why you get stuck with me talking about abandoned amusement parks and this book. How many three to four hours long car rides have you listened to my tangents? And it's all probably stuff that I've told you before, but you know my memory. I know you have the first draft of this book that I sent you years ago, and I hope you've enjoyed what it's evolved to now. You're my living teddy bear. Ich liebe dich!

Gabe and Gavin, my brothers, I still laugh that y'all are stuck with me. And y'all know what I want to call you both right now, but I'll spare you, especially Gavin (it's tempting). Thanks for putting up with me! You'll always entertain my weird endeavors and join along, and you both never make me fail to laugh. Gabe, any of the most morbid things in this book I have learned from you. Gavin, any of the most tart, cruel yet hilarious comments in this book I learned from you. Gavin, you're a fireball. Gabe, you're a man of few words. But, y'all are both hilarious, fire and ice. And for whatever reason, you both entertain me most often and probably tolerate other times. Thank you both for doing so! I'm glad y'all are stuck with me. Love y'all!

To Laurie, my godmother by choice, for some reason you seem to like having me as a daughter from another mother despite how weird I am. Maybe it's because you enjoy watching me harass Gavin. Nonetheless, thank you for loving me as I love you! You're also my cheerleader who feeds me black dyed burgers as you drove me to my job to play vampire, braves the madness that is Magic Kingdom NYE with me, and smuggles me tacos under my skirt as I worked the streets of England. I have three parents because of you. And you're not even obligated to be stuck with me. You've willingly listened to me go on about old school Epcot dark rides and the spontaneous ideas I've had for this story. Then now, I likely have you crying or tearing up. Sorry! Haha. But I love you! (and Floof)

To my grandparents Kepps and Granddaddy, Mary and Charles, I cherish you both more than you'll ever know. I think the wild country heart of Granddaddy probably finds my eccentric nature, and hair colors, funny if anything. The brutal sense of humor in our family comes right from you, Charlie Boy. It never fails to make us laugh. And on a serious note, I'll forever be in awe of you. You've had a wild life, I think wild is the best way to describe you, but for as wild as it was it's been the most inspirational. You're a lighthouse, your light shines in a way that through you, people come to know the Lord. The admiration and respect for you that I have will always be incredible. You are one of the greatest man I know, and I'm so blessed to call you my grandfather. Now, don't laugh at Kepps if she tears up in the next part. Kepps, you're a gem of an era forgotten. We're both old fashioned, old souls- and actually, now I recognize where that came from.

I'm not entirely sure how to put in to words, my mind is hit or miss. But I love you! You're an incredible woman who doesn't give herself a fraction of enough credit. You criticize yourself where there's absolutely nothing to criticize. I'm pretty sure you're what the 'grandmother gold standards' are based off of. You'll never understand the perpetual state of wanting to come and visit for as long as possible. I'm so, so glad to call you my Kepps. The world is a classier place because of you. I love the both of you forever and always. Y'all will eternally be a highlight of my life.

Romi, the talented and loveliest artist I know, you brought a part of my life to life in a way I've never been able to. When it comes to visual arts, I struggle with picturing much less actually executing that vision. Somehow, you tapped into my mind and created what I didn't know I wanted. You're always such a pleasure to work with and your art is far better than I could've dreamed for this story. Thank you so much for taking this on and making Masqueraded all the more special with your gift!

ABOUT THE AUTHOR

Alexis Dees is a lifelong creative writer and storyteller of all tales enchanting and unsettling. She focuses on stories that maintain a balance of whimsical fantasy, morbid darkness, and offbeat eccentricities... which sometimes ties into the matter of amusement attractions, an industry she's been involved with professionally for nearly ten years as an entertainer. As all sensible intellects do, instead of pursuing a traditional 9 to 5, she's ran away with the circus more than once; and when she's not tied up in aerial silks or reading the Brothers Grimm for the millionth time, she's likely traipsing about an abandoned amusement park.

If you're interested in her quirky nonsense, you can find her on Instagram, Twitter, Facebook, and Pinterest @carouselofchaos or www.carouselofchaos.com.

COMING SOON

Masqueraded: Act Two

Unmasked, untamed, and unapologetic. It's literally one hell of a homecoming for Estela Nannette Sinclair. But it's not her hell, it's theirs.

Lacrimosa Medina

The joy was gone, dead. No one mourned, no one paid respects. All fell silent upon her death sentence. Her rotting corpse became a public spectacle left bare to decay. She was nothing more than a morbid attraction, the skeleton beneath the Ferris wheel.

www.ingramcontent.com/pod-product-compliance
Lightning Source LLC
Chambersburg PA
CBHW060755310726
48980CB00002B/105

* 9 7 8 0 5 7 8 7 2 0 9 9 9 *